Critical accl.

Don't Be a Nice Girl
'Seamlessly plotted, sardonically told, seeded with jokes and surprises that go off with bright lights and the smell of gun smoke.' Philip Oakes, *Literary Review*

'Mr Scholefield is a very fine story-teller – a writer impressively at home with character and passion and atmosphere.' *New Yorker*

Threats & Menaces
'Scholefield serves up yet another wicked brew of sin and bitters.' *Sunday Times*

'Gripping and sobering in several dimensions.' *Observer*

'Scholefield retains his place in the front rank of English crime writers.' *Publishers Weekly*

Dirty Weekend
'So gripping that I was feverishly turning the pages till dawn.' Carla McKay, *Daily Mail*

Thief Taker

'Anyone wanting to feel the collar of the new-style fictional cop should read Alan Scholefield.' Andrew Hope, *Evening Standard*

Never Die in January

'Boils with wit – Scholefield is arguably the best writer working in the genre today, faster than Ruth Rendell and even more thought-provoking than P. D. James. Wonderful from start to finish.' Gary Dobbs, *Rhondda Leader*

'An excellent police novel; tough, tense and all too human.' Mike Ripley, *Daily Telegraph*

'Scholefield provides an object lesson in what can be packed into fewer than 200 raunchy pages.' John Coleman, *Sunday Times*

Don't Be a Nice Girl

Alan Scholefield was originally a journalist but became a full-time novelist in the early sixties. He is now the author of more than twenty novels, one of which, *Venom*, was filmed starring Nicol Williamson, Sarah Miles and Oliver Reed. He has also written screenplays, a stage adaptation of *Treasure Island*, and two thirteen-part adventure series for TV, as well as five suspense novels under the pseudonym of Lee Jordan. He is married to the novelist Anthea Goddard and has three daughters.

Don't Be a Nice Girl is the fifth in a series featuring Detective Superintendent George Macrae and Detective Sergeant Leopold Silver.

Also by Alan Scholefield

Alan Scholefield

Don't Be a Nice Girl

A Macrae and Silver Novel

PAN BOOKS

First published 1994 by Macmillan

This edition published 1996 by Pan Books
25 Eccleston Place, London SW1W 9NF
and Basingstoke

Associated companies throughout the world

ISBN 0 330 34297 5

1 3 5 7 9 8 6 4 2

A CIP catalogue record for this book is available from
the British Library

Phototypeset by Intype, London
Printed and bound in Great Britain

My thanks for his help go, as usual, to Detective Inspector Hugh Toomer, of the Metropolitan Police (Retired). Any mistakes are my own.

Chapter One

Ai
Ki
Do
Harmony
Energy
The Way.
And the most important of all was the Way.
That's what she had said.

*Anyone, she had said, could learn the techniques;
few the Way. And it was especially hard in this place.
But she must learn it, for they would certainly try to hurt
her. They might even kill her. It had happened before.*

*She said she would teach her the techniques and the
Way, and other disciplines too. She could never know
too many.*

*And she would be her friend; her special friend.
Then she could look after her while she was still there.
By the time she left she would have taught her all she
knew. That way she might survive.*

*And the first thing she had to learn was this: she
must never, never be a nice girl.*

Chapter Two

'Don't be a nice girl,' Macrae said to Frenchy. 'That's the whole bloody point. Kick 'em in the slats. Scratch their eyes out. I bet they don't teach you that at this gym place.'

'It's not a gym place!' Frenchy said. 'It's a proper hall with proper mats and they're teaching us proper.'

'Proper-ly.'

'Oh, shit, proper-le-e-e.'

They were in the small kitchen of Macrae's terraced house in a part of Battersea which had been semi-gentrified. The rest of it still bore the hallmarks of its seedy past and violent present – many of the shops wore security shutters over their windows dating from the riots of the eighties.

'You want some more toast?' Frenchy said.

He shook his head. 'I'm getting too bloody fat.'

He poured himself an extra cup of coffee and pushed his chair back. It groaned in protest. 'Hear that?'

She leaned back against the sink unit, drank her

2

own coffee and inspected him. If he was putting on weight, it was only a little. He had always been a big man, heavy in the head and neck with an air of barely controlled violence about him. The combination appealed to her.

'You wouldn't look good thin, George.'

Detective Superintendent Macrae felt in his pockets for a packet of slim cigars, took one out and inspected it without lighting it.

'It's all this home cooking.'

'I can always stop.'

'I didna say that.'

Frenchy was a large young woman with long legs and good high breasts that thrust provocatively against the thin fabric of one of Macrae's shirts, which was all she was wearing on this autumn morning.

'It's just that I've got out of the habit of this sort of life.'

'Don't you like it?'

'Of course I like it. Don't you?'

She did not reply immediately and he looked up at her, a frown on his heavy bull-like face.

'You don't need to ask.'

'That's no reply.'

'It's just—'

'What?'

'Oh, nothing . . .'

'For Christ's sake, *what*?'

'I'm not used to being a housewi— keeper. That's all.'

'I've said – you don't have to.'

'Don't go on, George.'

They had reached this point several times in the past weeks and both had backed off from a confrontation.

'What am I supposed to do? I can't sit and stare at the telly all day.'

'Look, you know as well as I do why it's this way. If you don't like it—'

'I can lump it! Is that it?'

'I didn't mean it that way, lassie. What I meant was . . .'

'Jesus, George, don't you understand anything? I like being here. I like living in your house. I like getting meals for you and doing the ironing. *But not all the time.* That's why I go to my classes. They get me out. I meet people.'

'Throwing people around a church hall doesn't sound much like friendship.'

'We don't hurt each other. And then we go for a coffee afterwards.'

'And all these women are taking karate, or whatever it is?'

'It's not karate it's aikido and we don't throw people around the hall. Well, not like you mean it. It's something to defend ourselves with, that's all. And it's based on principles of harmony and spiritual cultivation.'

'Spiritual what?'

'You wouldn't understand, George.'

'Sounds like a mothers' meeting. Listen, never mind the harmony. When the villain comes at you, harmony isn't going to stop him. Don't you remember that yob with Silver's girl? That was harmony. He said take off your pants and she did. And he cut her up anyway. What she should have done was use her car keys, a ballpoint, anything. Harmony, Christ.'

'You're just talking, George, making a noise. You don't know what it's like coming down a dark street at night wondering if someone's following. The Old Bill don't know no better than we do. I mean, they been telling us for years: Don't struggle. Give in. Lie back and think of Britain.'

'England.'

'OK, think of England. Now suddenly they're saying fight back. Use anything you can. But we can't carry mace and if we carry hairspray, just to use in case of an attack – then it's a weapon and illegal and we're the ones who're guilty. It's not right, George.'

'I know it isn't. And I never believed in this lie back stuff so—'

'Hang on . . . and they tell you to scream, don't they? But you know as well as me that when people scream everybody else scarpers in case they get involved.'

'Shout fire. People take notice of that. Shout fire and kick him in the balls. The point is: don't be a nice girl.' He rose. 'Well, I'm off.'

'George . . . hang on a sec.'

He looked at his watch.

'It won't take long,' she said.

'That sounds ominous.'

'It's money. I'm sorry to go on about it but I haven't lived without my own money since I was a kid.'

'I gave you a hundred quid less than a week ago.'

'I know. But I've had to do the shopping and I've had to buy the liquor. God, have you any idea how much you spend on drink?'

'Never mind about that. What about your bloody ju-jitsu or whatever it's called. How much does that cost?'

'Not all that much.'

'How much?'

'Twenty-five quid.'

'Jesus.'

'I pay that out of my own money. My savings. But they're gone now.'

'Gone?'

'You don't think we can live on what you've been giving me, do you? I've been adding a bit each week and it's still not enough.'

Macrae mashed his unlit cigar in the sink and threw it into the rubbish bin.

'I wouldn't ask, George, you know that, except . . .'

He stuck his hand in his pocket and came out with his wallet. He took out a thin wedge of ten-pound notes. 'That's all till pay day.'

6

He counted out forty pounds and gave it to her.
'That's it. There isn't any more.'

'Leo! Leo . . . wake up! Macrae's on the phone!'

Detective Sergeant Leopold Silver, peacefully
asleep in his own bed not more than couple of miles
from Macrae's house, came out of unconsciousness
like a shooting star. 'Wha'?'

'Only kidding.'

Zoe Bertram was standing over the bed in her
street clothes. Leo fell back against the pillows, confused, heart pounding.

'Don't ever do that,' he said.

'You wouldn't wake up.'

'How . . .? When . . . when did you get back? I
didn't hear you. I didn't—'

'I know you didn't. And the chain wasn't on the
door and the bolts weren't fastened. You're hopeless.'
She bent and kissed him. 'Good morning, darling.'

'How was Edinburgh?'

'Very Scottish.'

'It's supposed to be.'

'Twee Scottish. Tartan everywhere. Thistles.
Cairngorms. Sporrans. You name it.'

'Don't say things like that when Macrae's around.
How was the "creative" conference?'

'Creative. I'm going to have a shower. Come and
talk to me.'

He followed her into the bathroom and she slipped off her clothes. She'd been away nearly a week

at a conference run by her advertising agency. Since they had been living together this was one of the longest periods they had been separated and Leo wasn't used to it. His hands went out to fondle her fruity little breasts.

'Let me have my shower and then you can have your way with me. In the mean time be calm. Oh! I nearly forgot your pressie. Look in my case.'

He padded back to the bedroom. 'Wow!' he called. 'Shall I put it on?'

'That's what I bought it for.'

In a moment he was back in the bathroom. He pirouetted and flung out his arms. He was wearing a tartan jockstrap. 'Wow, indeedy!' Zoe said. 'That's what Scottish men wear under their kilts.'

'What's the tartan?'

'Hunting Fraser.'

'As if I needed reminding. Come to bed this instant.'

'If we were in America you'd have to get my permission in writing for this sort of thing.'

She was like an eel. Her body was thin and wiry with fleshy surprises. She had big brown eyes and high cheekbones and dark hair that fell around her face as she crouched on top of him. They made a handsome, if convoluted, pair.

'Miss me?' she said when they were lying in each other's arms.

'No. Not really.'

'Liar!'

'Anyway, how did you find out what Scotsmen wear under their kilts?'

'I asked.'

'I'll bet.'

She stretched luxuriously. 'There's no' a wee bed like it, as we say in the land of plaid. My God, Leo, there isn't, is there?'

'You mean for sleeping in or what?'

'There you go. In Edinburgh they would call you a cannegotian.'

'What the hell's that supposed to mean?'

'Ask Macrae.'

She got up, padded through to the kitchen and was soon back with two steaming mugs of coffee. She sat on the edge of the bed and the morning sun lit up a fine golden down on the side of her breast.

'So what's new with you and the Scotchman? Solved any good crimes lately?'

'Don't ever let Macrae hear you say Scotchman. Things have gone quiet. There's been a major blitz on prostitution by that imbecile Scales but Macrae says it's only window-dressing because our clear-up rate fell last month. He wants to look good so he's picking up prostitutes and druggies and dossers, that sort of thing.'

'I didn't think Macrae got mixed up in investigations like that.'

'He doesn't. And that's the problem. Give him a really nasty murder to get his teeth into and he's as happy as a baby with a rusk. He loves picking up stones and seeing what horrible mess lies underneath.'

'So he's unhappy, what's new?'

'When he's unhappy, I'm unhappy. He makes me nervous and unhappy in about equal measures. But he's worse this time. I mean more irritable and more bloody-minded than usual. If only the punters would start killing each other again!'

Chapter Three

Macrae walked to the end of his road and hailed a taxi. He had walked slowly, even his hand gesture to stop the cab was slow. He entered it slowly and gave an address in Fulham in measured tones. Nothing had been hurried. Right?

He sat where the driver was less likely to see him in the rear-view mirror, placed his fingers gently over his ears and listened to the inside of his head.

Thump-thump... pause. Thump-thump... pause.

His heart was doing it again. Each time it paused he had the sickening feeling that it would never start again. He was sweating and in spite of the chilliness of the morning he opened the window of the cab.

For the umpteenth time he told himself it was nothing to worry about; something he had eaten; something with a perfectly simple explanation.

And for the umpteenth time he didn't believe himself.

Once, crossing the Channel in heavy seas, he had experienced that common apprehension among passengers, the feeling that when the bow goes down and down and you think it will never come up again – it does. That was what his heart-beat was like.

It had started a couple of weeks ago, soon after he had met Bulloch at the Rake's Progress, a pub off Chancery Lane and a place Macrae went to when he wanted to drink unseen and undisturbed. He had taken Silver along with him.

It was a period when everything was suddenly quiet. People were not killing each other in what the Metropolitan Police called Eight Area and the general public Westminster. It stretched from Macrae's base at Cannon Row Police Station, along the river into Chelsea, across the parks to Bayswater and beyond, and it also took in Piccadilly Circus.

In several weeks not a head had been smashed in; there had not been a good old-fashioned strangling, not even a knifing.

Peace had broken out in Westminster and Macrae didn't care much for peace. He liked the hustle and bustle generated by murder. He liked the interrogation, the hunt for clues, the piecing together of the jigsaw. He liked drawing out of people little bits of the puzzle, bits they sometimes didn't even know they had.

But to Silver the big man's irritation and tension seemed to owe its genesis to something other than the temporary lack of murders.

He had clashed with almost everyone in the station as well as Deputy Commander Scales and

Detective Chief Superintendent Les Wilson, his own immediate guv'nor.

Macrae was always clashing with Scales and Wilson but he wasn't the kind of person who normally snapped at his junior officers.

It was just noon when he and Silver reached the Rake, which was still recovering from the night before. It was dimly lit and there was a smell of yeast and hops mixed with stale cigarette smoke. The barman had the etiolated look of a plant growing without sunlight.

'Dram and a pint,' Macrae said to the barman. 'What're you drinking, laddie?'

'Gin and tonic.'

Leo had learned the hard way. If he tried to keep pace with Macrae he would be legless in a matter of hours. But with a gin and tonic no one knew how much gin was in the glass and he could go on topping it up with tonic.

'Slainté.' Macrae threw the whisky back in one gulp and followed it by a pull on the ale. 'That's taken the taste of bloody Scales out of the mouth.'

'George! George Macrae!' A figure appeared from the shadows on the far side of the room. 'I thought I knew that voice.'

'Christ, guv'nor, it's yourself!'

'Aye, it is that.'

The two Scotsmen greeted each other warmly and Leo saw a man about Macrae's height but older and thinner. He might once have been as bulky as Macrae but now the skin hung on him in folds.

'This is Chief Superintendent Bulloch,' Macrae said to Silver. 'My old guv'nor in the Flying Squad and the best there ever was. What're you drinking, sir?'

'No, I'm all right.' He held up a Bloody Mary.

'You're looking fit, sir.'

'Thanks, George. I've taken off a bit of weight.'

'I haven't seen you since . . . it must have been that siege job in Eaton Square. The one with the poisonous snake in the house.' He turned to Leo. 'Mid-seventies. A kidnapping that went wrong in more ways than one. You remember reading about that, don't you?'

'Oh, yes,' Leo said. He did a quick mental calculation and estimated he would have been about five at the time.

'The guv'nor broke them. Just stood outside in the cold and broke them. Wasn't that so, sir?'

'Aye. You can always break filth like that if you hold on long enough.'

Macrae drained his glass and said, 'Come on, guv'nor, you're going to have one with me. What is it, a Bloody Mary?'

'No, no, just tomato juice.'

'Oh, come on, sir!'

'Tomato juice, George.'

Macrae turned to Silver but Leo held up a full glass. 'I'm OK.'

Bulloch said, 'That's the spirit, Sergeant, you don't want to start having a drink problem at this stage. Do you smoke?'

'Only sometimes, sir.'

'I'd give it up altogether if I were you. I have.'

Leo saw Macrae scowl into his glass then take out a slim Panatella and light it.

Bulloch tapped his chest. 'This is where the problem will be. Heart. You heard about my trouble, George?'

'Don't think so, guv'nor.'

'I thought you'd all have heard. About six months ago. Thought it was indigestion at first. You know, wind. But Christ! Well . . . I won't go into details but if they hadn't got me into intensive care in twenty minutes I'd have been a goner. Twenty minutes, George. Makes you think.'

'Aye, it does that.' Macrae turned to the barman. 'Gi' us a dram.'

Bulloch finished his tomato juice. 'Well, I've got to see my ladies. That's what I'm doing now. Going round to visit police widows. Let me tell you something. Teach your wife everything you can about the house, the car, the mortgage and how to do all the things a man usually does. Because one day your wife's going to be a widow, George, and she'll need to know how to change a fuse. I go round and try to cheer them up and some of them don't even know they've got to check the oil in the car. It's pathetic. They just sit at home staring out of the windows.'

He threw back his tomato juice. 'Nice to see you again.' He nodded to Leo and was gone.

Macrae stared down at the whisky glass in his hand. 'God Almighty,' he said. 'That was a really hard man. And look at him now!'

The taxi stopped at a tall and elegant terraced house in Fulham built of yellow brick with white window surrounds. A brass plate listed the names of three doctors. Macrae sat in the waiting room for twenty minutes then the buzzer sounded and he went into the surgery. Dr G. D. Kanwar was a small, middle-aged Indian, with delicate wrists and slender fingers. He looked up, frowned, smiled, stood up and held out his hand. 'Hello, George.'

'G.D.'

'I didn't realize you were the Macrae in the appointment book. Take a seat.'

As he sat down he could hear the muffled double-beat of his heart. It sounded like a funeral drum.

'It's quite some time since we last met,' Dr Kanwar said.

'They told me you weren't on the police rota any longer.'

'I had a friend who was a veterinarian. One winter's morning he found himself in the middle of a muddy field with his arm up to his shoulder in the rear orifice of a cow. He said to himself: "Do I want to be doing this?" So he became a solicitor. I felt the same way about being called out at three o'clock in the morning to examine someone whose throat had been cut.'

'You get used to it.'

'How's the curry cycle? I remember you were eating it hotter and hotter. Have you burst any abdominal capillaries? Is that what you've come to see me about?'

'No. I've just come for a check-up.'

Dr Kanwar sat back in his chair and smiled, showing a mouthful of extremely white teeth. 'A check-up?'

'I haven't had one for a while, G.D., and—'

The doctor held up his hand. 'George, that was just about perfect.'

'What was?'

'I don't see you for a long while. I'm not your regular doctor. And suddenly you appear out of the blue. So I ask myself, what does Superintendent Macrae want coming out all this way to see me? And you tell me: a check-up. It is the perfect Baliant Offer.'

'The perfect what?'

'About forty years ago a British psychiatrist, Michael Baliant, wrote about people like you; people who come to a doctor's surgery with headaches or for check-ups but really for something else. And they want the doctor to *discover* what it is. They want the doctor to tell them why they're there. So save me the trouble, George, why *are* you here?'

'My heart, G.D. It's all over the bloody place.

Seems to beat one minute and stop the next. And I get a pain here.' He indicated the centre of his chest.

'Slip off your top clothes and I'll have a look at you.'

Dr Kanwar gave him a thorough examination and at the end said, 'I know you used to drink a lot and smoke a lot. Still?'

'Well . . . I wouldn't call it a lot.'

'What about coffee?'

Macrae nodded. 'All coppers drink a lot of coffee.'

'Could be that. Too much coffee can irritate the ventricles. They begin to muddle up the messages from the pacemaker.'

'But I don't have a pacemaker!'

'Everybody has a pacemaker, a natural one.'

'Oh.'

'It's probably nothing much, but with your life-style we can't be sure. I'd give you an ECG but I don't do them in the surgery because the practice is too busy and there are a dozen experts round the corner. So just to make certain I'll give you a chit and you make an appointment at Fulham General. All right?'

'Fine.'

'You sound disappointed. Just be happy that the organ is beating at all. You've been destroying your-self for years and you're still around.' He stood up and handed Macrae the appointment slip. 'Go to the cardiac unit and give it to reception, they'll make an appointment. In the mean time, stop worrying.'

'Just live normally?'

'Except for the coffee and the booze and the fags.'

Macrae walked out into the autumn sunlight feeling like a ten-year-old. He wanted a drink. Live normally, G.D. had said. With exceptions of course. And stop worrying. But Bulloch had said they'd thought *his* was indigestion. Twenty minutes. Christ, what if—? He turned the corner in the direction of the hospital. He could compromise of course. There was always white wine. That wasn't a real drink, was it? But he didn't want to drink alone. He'd phone Silver. In the mean time he'd make the appointment.

'Another bottle?' Zoe pointed to the empty wine bottle. 'This one looks lonely, don't you think?'

They were having lunch in their favourite trattoria in Soho.

'Who's paying?' Leo said.

'My treat. I'm still on expenses.'

He ordered another bottle. They were having a meal they both loved: prosciutto with a very ripe Galia melon, then veal with lemon.

'What was the food like in Edinburgh?'

'Not bad if you like haggis, crowdie and bashed neeps.'

'Come on, they've got some good restaurants there.'

'Maybe. I didn't find one.'

The new bottle arrived.

'How's the family?' Zoe asked.

Leo looked up from his veal. 'Why?'

'What d'you mean, why? It's a civil question. Don't be so bloody touchy.'

'The usual. This time they've been fighting over a duvet.'

'A duvet? What's there to fight about?'

'You want to hear?'

'Of course. I love stories about duvets, blankets, carpets, old logs, gravel paths.'

'Mock not.'

She sat up, exaggeratedly attentive. Reports about Leo's family – an irascible argumentative, irritating group, half foreign, half English, who lived in a huge old flat on the wrong side of the Finchley Road – always made her wary. Leo was loyal to them in his own way. If she laughed immoderately he was likely to take umbrage but if she took him seriously he became tetchy at her incomprehension. She told herself it might have something to do with their Jewishness so she, being an agnostic – if not a full-blown atheist – couldn't be expected to understand them.

'I'm waiting,' she said.

The Case of the Hot Duvet had started some weeks before. Now it had become a family saga in which everyone was embroiled and about which everyone had an opinion.

'I want (*vant*) a duvet,' Manfred Silver, Leo's father, had said on the first cold day of the autumn.

Originally called Silberbauer before he anglicized his name, Manfred (short, portly, grey Vandyke beard, corduroy jacket) and his wife Lotte (plump, untidy) had left their native Austria and emigrated to England. Although they had lived most of their adult lives in London they still had their Austrian accents and still mangled their English syntax, usually in moments of high drama as when Manfred could not find a clean shirt or when his chess night was cancelled.

'I slept cold last night. Feel.' He placed his clean white hands against Lotte's neck.

'For God's *sake*, Manfy!'

'You see? How can I play with cold fingers?'

'Do you ever ask your pupils that question? That music room is the coldest room in the flat.'

As she spoke she tidied. She was always tidying the old-fashioned rooms with their high moulded ceilings, but it didn't appear to help. Each Sunday, when Leo, his sister Ruth, her husband Sidney Marcus and their son Stanley, gathered in the flat for lunch, it always seemed as though a high wind had recently blown through it.

'You want that the piano should vorp?'

'What is vorp?' Lotte asked. She tidied away the Sunday paper.

'Can I please have it back?' Leo said. 'I haven't finished reading it yet.'

'Sorry, my darling.' Lotte gave him the paper then ruffled the crisp black hair which sat against his skull like a cap. 'But please, Leo, feet.'

He was wearing what he usually wore; a black polo neck and black cords. His shiny black loafers had crept up on to the sofa.

'They're clean,' he said.

Manfred, who hated dirt of any kind, and who washed his hands after each piano lesson in case he caught something frightful from one of his pupils, said, 'How can they be clean? Nothing in London is clean. In the police force you go into urinals and stand in . . . in . . .'

'In the fire brigade they go into urinals. In the medical profession they go into urinals. Members of the London Symphony Orchestra have been known to go into urinals.'

'Don't be smart with your father. You know what I mean.'

'Anyway it's bad manners putting your feet on the sofa,' his sister Ruth said. 'I don't want Stanley learning bad manners.'

Ruth was some years older than Leo and usually dressed in flowing garments and wooden beadwork. She liked to give the impression of an earth mother but worried about getting fat.

Sidney, her husband, had discovered denim. His bald head rose out of a denim shirt and a denim jacket. His legs were encased in denim and his feet in orange cowboy boots. He had taken to wearing a gold chain which was considered trendy in the estate agency business. Manfred looked upon all this with dark suspicion.

Long ago Sidney had become apprehensive of the family into which he had married but he did his best to hide his nervousness by smiling a lot.

He sat now on the edge of one of the easy chairs. Stanley, his small son, was on the floor between his legs, colouring in by numbers.

'Anyway,' Lotte said to her husband, 'what is vorp?'

Manfred threw up his hands in despair. 'It is when the wood bends, you silly woman. You know what that Bosendorfer is worth now? Thousands upon thousands. I put heating in that room, pretty soon it looks like a banana.'

'Bananas stop cramp,' Sidney said. 'It's the potassium.'

The family faces turned towards him like a cluster of radar dishes. He smiled at them. 'It's true.'

Manfred pursued his original thought. 'When I was a little boy in Vienna I had a duvet.'

'Mödling is *not* Vienna! It is *outside* Vienna!' Lotte said. 'And in those days we slept with windows open and the heating off. We needed such things.' She turned to Ruth and Leo. 'Such lovely duvets. Down feathers from eider ducks. And every morning the maids shook all the feathers to the bottom of the covers and put them in the open windows. All over the Cottäge, where we lived in Vienna, people put their duvets in the windows to get the air on dry days.'

'The doctor's daughter! The Cottâge! Maids!' her husband said.

Those were the opening salvos in Manfred's campaign for a duvet. Once he had brought it up he did not let the subject drop for more than a day or so, and gradually, like Chinese water torture, it wore Lotte down.

Zoe listened to this story with wide eyes and a half smile. 'Well?' she said. 'Has he bought one?'

'I don't know. But he's still threatening to.'

There was a discreet buzzing in Leo's pocket. He took out a small mobile phone and spoke for a moment under the withering glare of other diners.

Hastily he put the phone away. 'That was Macrae,' he said. 'I've got to go.'

Chapter Four

Macrae shoe-horned his bulk into the passenger seat of Silver's VW Golf and said, 'It took you long enough.'

'The traffic's solid at Hyde Park Corner, guv'nor.'

Macrae grunted.

'Back to the station?' Leo asked.

'No. I want a drink. Let's go to the Rake.'

Leo drove along the Fulham Road in slow traffic and Macrae said, 'Where the hell were you anyway?'

'Zoe was buying me lunch at a trattoria in Soho.'

'A tratt-or-ia was it? And what did you have in this tratt-or-ia?'

'Prosc—' Leo checked himself. He didn't think Macrae was in the mood for pretentious foreign words. 'Smoked ham and melon. And then veal with lemon washed down with a couple of bot—'

Macrae's stomach gurgled alarmingly. 'I want something to eat and a glass of white wine. Don't you know anywhere around here?'

Leo could hardly believe his ears. Once, early in their relationship, he had ordered a white wine and soda. Macrae's face had darkened and he had said, 'That's a girl's drink.'

'There's a wine bar down on the river called Mallard's. They serve decent food.'

'A wine bar!'

Macrae also hated wine bars on the grounds that the tables were too close together but Leo knew that he had once been patronized in one when they were on a job in Cambridge. Macrae had ordered malt whisky and named Glenmorangie only to be told by the proprietor that funnily enough they only served wine. It was a wine bar, you see. Perhaps he hadn't understood that.

'This one's all right, guv'nor, the tables are well spaced and the steak's good.'

'That's what I want, a good steak.'

They turned into Sydney Street in the direction of Chelsea and the Thames. A short line of traffic had built up at the intersection with the King's Road. Leo's view was blocked by a food truck but there was just enough room to squeeze past it and make a double line at the intersection. He swung out and put his foot down. As he passed the cab on the truck he saw an arm waving violently. Then, too late, he saw a small car coming out of a side street ahead of the truck. He saw a woman's terrified face. He slammed on the brakes. The car slid. There was a sharp crunching noise and everything stopped.

'Oh, Christ!' Macrae said.

'Didn't you see my fucking signal!' the truck

driver shouted. 'You had to fucking pass me, didn't you!'

Macrae said softly to Leo, 'Let me handle this.' He went to the woman. 'You all right, love?'

She had got out of her car. Macrae estimated her age at about thirty. She was small and fair and dressed in a dark blue track suit and white trainers.

'I think so.' Her dark glasses had fallen on to the road. She bent to pick them up and staggered slightly.

'Let's get your car out of the way,' Macrae said.

He and Leo pushed it against the kerb. The line of traffic moved into the King's Road. A few passersby who had stopped to stare saw there was no blood or broken bones, nothing much really, and went on their way.

'God, I'm sorry,' Leo said to the woman. 'I thought the truck driver was waving me on.'

She smiled. It was a rueful smile, yet it lit up her face. 'And I thought he was waving *me* on.'

The truck driver had joined them. 'You're right, miss, I *was* waving you through.'

He was a thick-set man in his forties with a pale freckled face and a fringe of light red hair on an otherwise bald pate. He was dressed in blue coveralls and dirty sneakers.

He stuck his angry face into Leo's. 'You must be blind, mate!'

Leo reached for his warrant card to identify himself.

27

Macrae's large hand came down on his arm.

Macrae turned to the truck driver and said, 'Mind your own business, laddie.'

'Mind my business!' He was outraged.

Macrae turned to the woman. 'Are you sure you feel OK?'

She was holding on to the roof of her car. 'I'm . . . I'm a little dizzy.'

'Listen, Fulham General's just around the corner. We'll take you there, then we'll come back and look after the car.'

He helped her into the front passenger seat. Leo got into the back.

'Hang on! Hang on!' The truck driver gave the woman a piece of paper. 'You have any trouble, you want a witness, you can get me here. Take it. It's got my name and address.'

'Thank you . . . I don't think . . . thank you . . .'

Macrae started the car, made a U-turn, and shot back along Sydney Street in the direction of the hospital he had so recently left.

'Are you all right, lassie?' he said.

She was touching a swelling on the side of her head and did not reply.

'We'll have you there in a few minutes.'

A voice erupted on the police radio. 'Zebra Bravo . . . Zebra Bravo . . . will any vehicle in the vicinity of the Brompton Oratory—'

Macrae flicked the radio off. 'Nearly there,' he said.

He parked in the reserved space for ambulances. One was unloading a man on a trolley, a nurse was holding a drip above his head. Macrae pushed past, saw a wheelchair and came back with it.

'In you get.'

'I'm—'

'Don't talk. Just sit back.'

He wheeled her into casualty. A nurse said, 'What've you got there?'

'Traffic accident. She's had a bump on the head.'

'Right, give her to me. Don't go away.'

She took the wheelchair and went down a narrow passage finally disappearing through swing doors. Macrae walked back to the car.

A porter said, 'Can't you read? Ambulances only. I've got a good mind to clamp you.'

Macrae felt like picking him up and throwing him bodily in front of the traffic on the Fulham Road but he'd had enough excitement for the time being. 'I'm sorry, I don't speak English,' he said, then drove to the parking area, leaving the porter staring after him in confusion.

As he and Leo walked back to casualty, Leo said, 'Where the hell did she *come* from? I mean, there was no one. A clear road, then suddenly—'

'From behind the bloody truck, that's where she came from. She'd no right to come through a line of traffic. So don't you go blaming yourself. It was *her* fault.'

'Maybe we shouldn't have brought her ourselves. Maybe we should have called an ambulance.'

'You must be soft in the head. What happens if you call an ambulance to a road accident?'

'I'm not sure I— Oh, yes, I see. They have to report it to the traffic police.'

'Right. And what would happen then?'

'I'd be breathalysed.'

'Right. Do you think you'd have passed?'

Leo paused.

'How many bottles did you and Zoe have?'

'Two. No, I wouldn't have passed. But what if she—?'

'Listen, she could walk and talk. There's no problem. Just you forget about that.'

Leo walked in silence for a few yards then stopped again. 'It wasn't my fault.'

'Hang on to that, laddie.'

'I mean she came from nowhere, from bloody nowhere.'

'Right.'

'Look, guv'nor, I'm sorry about this but I wasn't drunk. I really wasn't. OK, I might not have been able to pass a breathalyser but I'd driven all the way out to Fulham without a problem.'

'I know you're not drunk. So snap out of it.'

'She came out right in front of me. Just like that. From nowhere!'

Chapter Five

'Conferences . . . meetings . . . Jesus Christ, that's all we do these days. Chairman Scales and his bloody conferences. It's more like ICI or IBM than the Met.'

'Keep it down, George.'

They were in Detective Chief Superintendent Wilson's office.

Wilson said, 'Anyway, you've got nothing better to do, the punters aren't killing each other.'

'I don't like meetings. I don't like joint decisions. I don't like Scales.'

Macrae was speaking through a mouthful of canteen sandwich. Not quite the steak he'd been looking forward to. He washed it down with a machine-made, styrofoam-encased liquid which went under the guise of coffee.

Thump-thump . . . pause . . . Thump-thump . . . pause . . .

Coffee could cause it, G.D. had said. So what was he supposed to drink? The tea that came out of the machine was even worse.

He would cut down. Of course he would. He'd

cut down on coffee and the booze and the cigars. But he couldn't give them up entirely. They'd be wanting him to give up sex next. There came a point, he told himself, where you could be giving up too much; when what was left of your life wasn't worth getting out of bed for.

Thump-thump . . . Come on . . . COME ON!

He threw the rest of the sandwich into the waste-basket and drained the coffee. 'Let's go, Les.'

The station waiting-room was full of smelly dossers and angry-looking tarts, as it had been for days.

'God Almighty,' Macrae said. 'It's worse than Cardboard City.'

Scales was sitting under the non-smoking logo which was painted on the wall above his desk. Macrae usually took out his cigars on principle once he entered and forced the deputy commander to ask him to desist. It was a tiny victory. But today he hadn't the heart – which was a silly phrase in the circumstances.

Sitting there with his bony skull covered by thin strands of long hair, Scales reminded Macrae of pictures he had once seen of the dead elders of a south-east Asian tribe. Relatives kept the dried corpses about the house in a kind of family unit. The difference was that Scales was alive, you could hear him clicking his ballpoint pen far down the corridor.

'Les . . . George . . .' he said. 'Have a pew.'

Wilson and Macrae sat down in straight-backed

chairs, the legs of which had been shortened by an inch or two to make them lower than Scales' desk chair.

The deputy commander leaned back. 'Well?' he said. They stared at him: Wilson intently, Macrae contemptuously. 'What are we going to do?'

'About what, sir?'

'About the damned report.'

'Which report?' Macrae asked. There had been so many reports recently: governmental committee reports, inter-departmental reports, reports from the desk sergeant about people who removed stamp pads from his drawers, reports about the state of the lavatories, about the state of the carpets, even about the state of the potted plants.

'The Sheild Report. I should have thought you'd have registered that, George.'

'If it's true it recommends getting rid of paper pushers and nearlymen, then I'm not against it. I've never believed in jobs for life.'

'You might be under threat yourself if they did away with that.' Scales said it lightly, a skeletal smile on his thin lips, but the smile belied the depth of meaning and the dislike behind it.

Scales disliked almost everything about Macrae; if he had to sum up his reasons they would be encapsulated in the simple phrase 'his attitude', by which he meant to life, to the police, to his colleagues, to women. Scales knew he benefited from Macrae's ability as an old-style thief-taker, but on balance he'd rather have him out of Cannon Row and out of the police force entirely.

Macrae knew this and so did Wilson.

They discussed the Sheild Report for a while then Scales moved on to his favourite complaint: private telephone calls made from the station. Macrae and Wilson had heard it a dozen times. Finally Macrae broke in and said, 'I'd like to enter my own complaint.'

Scales looked as though he had been struck in the face. 'What's that?'

'The station's like a madhouse. We've got these filthy dossers and a line of tarts all along the corridor It's disgusting.'

Scales clicked his pen. 'I want you to think about something. The major complaint about the police is the clear-up rate. People say we've got computers, fast cars, we've got the manpower, yet when Mr and Mrs Public walk down the street they're harassed by beggars, they have to step over dossers, then they're importuned by female *and* male prostitutes. But the Home Office says go after the big criminals. All right, we do. But we can't do that at the expense of quality of life. Clean up London, that's what we have to do. Clean it up and keep it clean.'

Macrae yawned. They would have half an hour of this now. He let his mind wander to the accident earlier. Wouldn't Scales like to know about that! And wouldn't he be disappointed to discover that George Macrae hadn't been drinking and driving. Wouldn't that be a nice irony.

When they left Scales' office he and Wilson walked down the corridor and a new load of tarts were milling about in the charge office. A voice said, 'Hello, George.'

He saw a face he might once have known. An attractive young girl said, 'How's Frenchy?'

Macrae ignored her and the laughter that followed him.

Wilson said, 'I want a word, George. Not here, in the old building.'

Cannon Row Police Station comprised two buildings, a tall red-brick Victorian structure and a new high-tech box. The two buildings were joined umbilically top and bottom. They entered the old building and Macrae followed Wilson upstairs to the top floor where he unlocked a door marked Store Room. They entered a small dusty office with a desk and a couple of chairs. Wilson locked the door behind him.

Macrae said, 'Where's the monk doing the illuminated manuscript?'

'They were going to use this for storage but when it didn't happen I got the key.'

Wilson opened the desk drawer, took out a bottle of whisky and two glasses. He poured a couple of stiff shots and said, 'Cheers.'

Macrae looked at the whisky. He could feel his heart beating erratically. A couple of drinks wouldn't make it any worse, he supposed. Anyway, wasn't whisky supposed to be good for the heart?

'Have you read the Sheild Report?' Wilson said.

'Only what it says in the press.'

'Then you'll know what they're going to do about chief superintendents.'

'They'll never axe you. Never.'

'George, the whole bloody rank's going, or will go.'

'Don't you believe it. I've seen reports like this before. So have you. Fixed-term contracts: remember those? They dropped that idea quickly enough. And work-related pay: they dropped that too. You don't need to worry, Les, no one's going to knock out a whole rank.'

'But what if they do?'

'You always said you wanted to live in Spain.'

'On what?'

'There'll be a golden handshake.'

Wilson shook his head. 'Maybe. George, you've got some contacts in the private sector. Office security; that sort of thing.'

'Do you really want to work in private security?'

'I've got a mortgage to pay. And Beryl likes holidays in the sun.'

'I wouldn't worry about it yet. Wait till it happens.'

'Put the word out, George.'

Wilson lifted the whisky bottle and Macrae put his hand over his glass. 'I'm trying to cut down.' He finished what he had left and rose.

Wilson said, 'One thing more. Keep an eye on Frenchy.'

'What's that supposed to mean?'

'Exactly what it says. You know what would happen if Scales found out.'

'We've been through this before, Les.'

'Living with a known prostitute. Sorry, but it's the only phrase I know to describe it – and it's the official one. Nothing could save you if he found out.'

'That's why she's not working. Companion. Girl friend. Common-law wife. Take your pick. And there's nothing in police regulations which says we shouldn't live together.'

Wilson looked up at him without smiling. 'I hope that's true.'

Driving home in the windy darkness the phrases kept tumbling around in Macrae's head. *Living with a known prostitute.* He didn't like that one but it was true enough. Not now, of course. Now she was what he had described her as: a companion – or what did they call it now: a partner?

Christ, who would ever have thought that the wispy little thing he had first seen in a squat in Holloway would turn out to be Frenchy, his bloody partner. He doubted whether she would ever have described herself as a 'partner', she wasn't the sort who allowed semantics to govern her life; she lived it depending on how she was feeling.

He drove along the Embankment and the image of the woman he had met those years ago seemed suddenly very close.

He knew now, of course, what her background was, but he hadn't known then. It had been that dismal storyline which so often accompanied women like Frenchy in London. The break with home usually started it, and for her that had been when her mother had married for the third and last time.

Frenchy had never had any hesitation in describing her past and this is what made her special, he thought. With what had happened to her, one might have expected an introverted neurotic, instead she was extrovert, ebullient and optimistic – and perfectly counterbalanced Macrae, who was very much his own man and a pessimist to boot.

He wondered, as he approached Battersea Bridge, what a psychotherapist would have made of Frenchy in those days. Screwed her up for life probably.

She'd been around sixteen then and had recently left home to take up with a drummer in a pop group. From what Macrae gathered this was caused more by what was happening at home than the drummer's attractions. Her mother's third husband was a cheap little villain who filled the house with men who kept trying to trap Frenchy in the upstairs bedrooms.

So she'd left to live with her first real boyfriend. He was a few years older than she was and was already on heroin. They lived in a squat in Holloway.

From time to time, she had told Macrae, she felt excited and liberated by her experience, but most of the time she hated the squalor and the drugs.

But she was loyal. Donnie played the occasional

gig, but was doing half a gram of heroin a day. It was winter; the squat was damp; some of the windows were broken. Donnie got bronchitis. There was no money for food, no money for drugs, so she earned it the only way she could.

In his police career he had met many women who had gone on the game for a bloody good reason. Kids were involved or a husband or whole families whom they wanted to keep together. He had sometimes thought that they had better lives than his own mother had before she was found floating face down in the Findhorn, having endured life with his father just as long as she could.

Macrae was in the Murder Squad when he'd first met Frenchy. There had been a call to say there'd been a killing in a squat in Holloway.

Wrong information. There was a dead body, but no killing. The body was Donnie's and he'd died of a combination of drugs and pneumonia. When Macrae arrived Frenchy, thin and ghostlike, had been sitting by the body.

All she wanted was enough money to bury him and she'd said to Macrae: 'You want a fuck? It's only a tenner.'

He'd never forget that, nor the dreadful room.

'The parish will bury him,' he said. 'I'll see to it.'

They buried Donnie a few days later and that, Macrae had thought, was that.

But over the years he kept bumping into her. He met her again when he did a stint in the Vice Squad.

She remembered him but he hadn't recognized her. She'd grown, put on weight, matured.

The next time he saw her she was working for a pimp called Rambo who was one of his informants. It was just after he and his second wife had split up and he was needing a woman. So he phoned Rambo and asked for her.

'It's on the house, Mr Macrae,' Rambo had said. 'You'll like her.'

And he had.

They had liked each other.

It had developed from there.

Macrae pulled up outside his house. The windows were dark, the place deserted.

The London Towers was in Ebury Street. If you were kind you said it was in Belgravia, if not, Victoria. It was a mid-priced hotel meant for businessmen whose companies wouldn't stand the strain of the Inn on the Park or the Royal Kensington. The London Towers was a regular for her. Or at least it had been in the past.

She paid off the cab on the opposite side of the street and studied the layout for a moment. The doorman was standing on the front steps rubbing his hands and moving his feet to keep the circulation going. It was such a characteristic pattern of behaviour among doormen that she had seen it even on the hottest days of summer.

The street was quiet and the hotel was quiet. She crossed over and said, 'Hello, love.'

The doorman was elderly and his eyesight in the glow of the street lights was not of the best. He came towards her, then said, 'God, it's Frenchy! I ain't seen you for an age.'

'A few months anyway. How're you keeping, Joe?'

'Mustn't complain.' He looked at the long legs encased in thigh boots, the skirt as big as a handkerchief, the see-through blouse, the flight bag on her shoulder. 'You here to work? Listen, we got a new manager. Very hot on you know what and I don't want to lose me job. Plus I haven't seen Rambo lately – if you know what I mean.'

'I don't work with Rambo no more. Things were getting too hot for him with all this police aggro so he's moved down to Portsmouth.'

'So who're you working with?'

'Lysander Goater.'

'The fake parson?'

'He's all right,' Frenchy said. 'And he'll see you right too. If he doesn't, I will.'

'OK, I could use a bit extra. You go round the side and I'll let you in. Use the stairs.'

In a moment she was in the hotel and climbing the emergency staircase to room 307. The place was cold and bleak and smelled of damp concrete and she wished she hadn't come. She hadn't done a trick for some months and she wasn't pleased to be back on the game. But things couldn't go on as they were. She told herself that what she was doing now would save her relationship with George, whereas living with him full time, skimping and scraping and trying to save a bit here and a bit there, would put it in jeopardy and probably end it.

She thought of Lysander Goater. She'd known him for some years and he'd always wanted her to leave Rambo and work for him but she'd remained loyal. Now things were different, and she could see what she'd been missing. Rambo was the sort of bloke who wrote the punter's name on the back of a match book, a hit-or-miss sort of person; not so Lysander. She'd spent a couple of hours with him earlier that day and was dead impressed.

For one thing Lysander had an elegant apartment near Hyde Park which he used as an office and for another he worked on a computer. While not computer literate, she was able to appreciate the organizational power it gave him. He brought up on the screen girls' names, complete with biographies, work details and which skills they had acquired.

He had been wearing a dark suit with a white clerical collar. It was not possible to regard him as just another pimp. She'd had brushes with 'Yardies' – the West Indian drug mafia who also sometimes ran girls – who had frightened the life out of her.

But although Lysander's pigmentation was similar to theirs, that's where it ended. He was small, gentle, clever and amusing. His father had been in the British Army although the family had originally come from a place called Zambia in Africa. Frenchy had no idea where this was. If the truth were told she had only a hazy idea where Africa was.

But, as Macrae had observed, anyone could be a brain surgeon, few could give the pleasure Frenchy gave.

So she didn't think of Lysander as a pimp at all and indeed he didn't think of himself as one.

'The word is "agent",' he had said. 'I am your agent and you are my client and you will be doing modelling.'

That was a new one for her. When Rambo sent her out there had been no disguising what she was there for, nor who the client was. Now she was a model. She was going to model lingerie, and Lysander gave her the money to go out and buy some. It made everything more interesting and more of a challenge.

They talked about the different types of gentlemen who might require her services. Frenchy usually described herself as an all-rounder who preferred straight sex. They discussed various groups and agreed that the Japanese, with their irregular copulatory rhythms and their penchant for poking about in the girls' bags, bringing out pieces of equipment and saying, 'I no pay extra for this . . . I no pay extra for that . . .' were the oddest.

And this led naturally to the codes.

'As you know,' Lysander said with winning

43

sincerity, 'gentlemen are sometimes rough and I don't want you to get hurt, I don't even want you to be frightened. So this is what we do . . .' And he told her certain words to use when she telephoned which would indicate her situation.

She had to phone when she went into the premises she had been sent to. It was a call which would acknowledge the fact that in her opinion everything was under control. Afterwards, she must phone again, but only once she was clear of the premises and safe.

Lysander gave her a small folding cell-phone. She had never possessed one before. Rambo had not gone in for phone calls and code words.

There was to be a strict time limit of one hour for each visit. If the gentleman required another hour she had to phone and say so. If she didn't phone, Lysander would put Plan B into operation: a rescue for which he would call in 'the boys'.

'One day you must meet the boys,' he said. 'I try to see as little of them as I can. If I may paraphrase the Iron Duke: I don't know what they do to the customers but they scare the hell out of me.'

Frenchy thought he was probably quoting from some recent movie and smiled dutifully. She imagined the Iron Duke might be a pop singer.

Pondering on these matters she reached the third floor of the London Towers and went along the carpeted corridor to 307. Lysander had made her feel part of a team with a backup organization and that helped to overcome her sense of *déjà-vu*. He hadn't mentioned Macrae though Frenchy was aware that the two of them knew each other. So she hadn't either. If Lysander didn't know she had been living with Macrae, so much the better.

She knocked at the door and a male voice called, 'Come in.'

He was a big man with a moustache that drooped on either side of his lips and fleshy jowls. The room was in semi-darkness. He was sitting on the bed, already half undressed. She noticed that he was wearing a purple vest. She hated purple vests.

'Come in . . . come in . . . come in . . .' he said.

She closed the door behind her.

'Hi,' he said. 'My name's Jimmy.'

'I'm Arlene.' ('They like fancy names,' Lysander had said. 'We'll call you Arlene.')

He put out his hand. She took it and he drew her towards him. The light fell on her face and she saw what she thought was a flash of recognition in his eyes.

'Do I know you?' she said.

'No, love. We've never done it before. It's my first visit to London.'

But she was cautious now. 'Always ask for ID,' Lysander had said. When she did the man said, 'What for?'

'I like to check.'

'Listen, the money's there. Take it.'

He lifted a bundle of notes from the bedside table and offered it to her.

She backed away. 'What's that for?'

'What d'you think it's for? Come on, let's do it. I can't wait any longer.'

'Do what? Why d'you think I'm here?'

'Don't give me that crap. We both know why you're here. Get your clothes off.'

'If you think I'm here for sex you're mistaken. It's not what you were told on the phone.'

'To hell with what I was told.'

'I'm a model. I model lingerie.'

He was becoming agitated. 'Now listen—'

She held up her hand. 'I've got to make a phone call. My agent. I've got to check in.' She smiled at him.

'Hurry up, then.'

She took her phone from her bag and dialled Lysander's number. The codes covered dangerous customers and also the Vice Squad.

When Lysander asked if everything was kosher, Frenchy said, 'Yeah, fine. Has William been in?' William was the code for the police. The Old Bill. 'If he comes in, tell him to leave the package.'

Lysander said, 'Have you checked his ID?'

'William doesn't have any.'

'Hey,' the punter said. 'Come on.'

Lysander said, 'Has he asked you to have sex?'

She smiled at the big man again. 'Oh, yes, he's great.'

Lysander said, 'Get out of there fast and for God's sake don't take any money.'

She put the phone in her flight bag. 'What was

all that about?' he said. 'And who the hell's William? I'm paying you to concentrate on me.'

'My brother.'

'To hell with your brother, let's have sex.'

'I told you I'm just here to model and that's all I'm going to do.'

He pushed the money at her. 'All right, you model. Nudge, nudge, wink, wink. And I'll pretend I've got a camera. But let's do the modelling in bed.'

She moved towards the door. If she could reach the corridor he would hardly be likely to chase her in his underwear.

As though sensing this he moved quickly to get between her and the door.

She pulled out her phone and said, 'Stay where you are. I'm a policewoman and you've been offering me money for sex.'

'What?'

'You're a . . .' but the phrase *agent provocateur* was beyond her. 'You're a . . .'

She swung her flight bag. It caught him on the side of the head and he overbalanced on to the bed. In a flash she had the door open but he bounced up and caught her. His mouth was open, his eyes looked almost demented. She felt his hand on her breast. The nails dug in. She yelled, then bit his arm. He recoiled. She broke loose and ran down the corridor.

'You bitch!' he called after her. 'I know who you are!'

She ran down the emergency stairs into Ebury

Street and on into Buckingham Palace Road. She found a phone booth. Her right breast was bleeding. She put tissues on the scratches then she phoned Lysander and told him what had happened.

'Go home,' he said.

'I can't. The bastard's a cop. I think he's at Cannon Row. He knows who I am.'

'Come in then. I'll think of something.'

Chapter Six

'The dentist says he's worried about one of my teeth.'
Zoe put her finger into her mouth and touched the
malign tooth. 'Uh . . . ear . . . ae . . . uh . . . bae . . .'

Leo had just come in and was standing at the
window looking out at the night sky above the roof-
scape of Pimlico.

'His name is Mr Nottage,' Zoe said. 'And I have a
vision of Mr Nottage lying by the side of his lady
wife having just made love and in that post-coital
state she says to him, "You're looking very pensive,
dear." And he replies, "I'm worried about Zoe
Bertram's upper right three." '

Leo did not respond.

'Don't you think that's funny?'

'Not really.'

'What's the matter with you? Ever since you
walked in you've been glomming around the place.
All I'm trying to do is cheer you up. You haven't
been caught taking bribes, have you?'

'For Christ's sake!'

'What then?'

'It's something that happened this morning.'

'D'you want a glass of wine?'

'God no!'

'OK, I'll be quiet.'

He told her about the accident. As he spoke her face twisted into a frown. 'But it wasn't your fault.'

'That's what Macrae said.'

'He's right.'

Leo began to pace up and down the long sitting-room.

'It's the sort of thing you expect to happen to Macrae, not me,' he said. '*He's* the sort of person who drinks and drives.'

'But you weren't drunk.'

'D'you know how much we had?'

'Not all that much.'

'OK. Camparis to start with and then *two* bottles of Chardonnay. There was no way I was going to pass a breathalyser.'

'But she cut into a line of traffic. You were within your rights.'

'I know I was. But it doesn't change things. I hit her and she's hurt and she's in hospital. And I'd been drinking.'

'But she walked to your car. And she spoke. She can't be badly hurt.'

'Apparently bangs on the head can have odd effects.'

He described what had happened when the doctor talked to them. He was a young man with flecks of blood on his white coat and a face haggard with exhaustion.

'We're keeping her overnight,' he said. 'At the moment it looks like a simple case of concussion, but we'll just make sure. We may give her a brain scan if we're not happy.'

Leo said to Zoe, 'A brain scan!'

'They haven't said so positively. Did you find out her name?'

'It's Laura. Laura Parkes. She has an address in Putney.'

'Have you checked how she is?'

'I did earlier and she was resting. I was almost too scared to in case . . . well . . . in case she'd—'

'Died? Don't be ridiculous. She had a bump on the head, that's all. Stop over-reacting. You're a detective sergeant. You're supposed to have seen everything. This is your background coming out. Your family over-dramatizes everything. You shouldn't be in the police at all.'

'Lucky for you I was.'

He was referring to her narrow escape from a rapist. He had arrested the man and later had supported her emotionally. They had been together ever since.

He said, 'Macrae saved me. If I'd taken my warrant card out that lorry-driver would have gone for me. He'd have had the traffic boys there and I'd have been blowing into the—'

'Leo, stop it! You were not at fault. She came out

of a side street into the line of traffic. Why don't you check again? Then you'll feel better.'

He made the call then said, 'The ward sister says she's been asking for me.'

'Why?'

'I don't know. I wish I did. But I think I'd better go and find out. You want to come?'

'No, you go and hold her hand by yourself.'

Leo drove the Golf, now looking slightly the worse for wear, first to Victoria Station to buy some flowers, then to the Fulham General. Laura Parkes was behind screens in the Lady Churchill ward. He came on her unexpectedly and was able to look down at her before she realized he was there. He hadn't really looked at her that morning. She was just a figure in a track suit and trainers, someone who had entered his life dramatically and who might be a problem. That – i.e. the problem – was fortunately behind him, for no one could now mention drinking and driving. But the moral imperative was unresolved.

She was dozing and lay as a child might lie, one hand flung out, the other touching her hair. She wasn't conventionally pretty, but there was a soft innocence about the relaxed face that he had seen in paintings of Renaissance madonnas. Her chestnut hair was spread out on the pillow and he recalled it had been tied back in a pony-tail that morning. She had a skin of translucent whiteness and he could see the regular throb of a pulse in the veins of her temple. There was an ugly yellow bump on her forehead.

Her eyes snapped open. They were large and the colour of washed denim.

'I'm Leo,' he said.

She smiled. 'I hoped you'd come.'

'I wanted to see how you were and say how sorry I am.'

'No, you mustn't apologize. It was my fault, it really was.' Her voice, like her face, was soft, but the timbre was deep.

He thrust out the flowers.

'Thank you, they're lovely.' She put them on the bedside cabinet. She was wearing a hospital night-dress which fell away and Leo was vouchsafed a spectacular view of two high, firm breasts.

'I'm Laura,' she said.

'Yes, I know.'

'I couldn't remember my name for a while.'

'The doctor in casualty said you had concussion. Do you remember us driving you to the hospital?'

'Us?'

'There was another man with me.'

'I only remember you. At least I think I do. It's difficult to tell now that you're here. I'm placing you in the frame so to speak. But whether I really remember you or not, I don't know.'

They talked for another few minutes then a nurse arrived and said visiting hours were over. Laura said formally, 'It was good of you to come.'

'I'm glad I did. Oh, and your car's been taken back to your flat in Putney.'

'I'm grateful. Was there much damage?'

'A dent in the driver's door. I want to pay for that.'

'Don't be silly. It was *my* fault. What about your car?'

'It's fine.'

'Really fine?'

'Really. I'll show you tomorrow. I'll take you home if they let you out.'

'There's no need. I can get a cab.'

'Nonsense. I'd like to.'

'Nothing happened,' Lysander Goater said to Frenchy. 'No money changed hands. You didn't get into bed with the client. There's no problem.'

They were in Goater's office, with the computer screen's cursor winking at them. Frenchy didn't think he was getting the point.

'He was a copper. A detective. I think I've seen him before. Anyway, I'm sure he's seen me.'

'You can't get locked up for being seen.'

'But I mean at Cannon Row. That's where I think he works. And that's where my – that's where Mr Macrae works.'

She didn't think it right when speaking to Goater to refer to Macrae as George. There were proprieties to be observed.

'Aah, that does put a different complexion on it. Let me think.'

He sat for a few moments, thinking, while Frenchy watched him.

'Right. I've thought. What you're saying is that under present circumstances if you go back and live with Mr Macrae you're afraid that he might be compromised, is that it?'

'They'll get him for living with a . . . well, with me. And they could kick him off the Force. I wouldn't mind for myself but what would Mr Macrae do? He lives for the police.'

'*De gustibus*,' Lysander said, putting the tips of his slender black fingers together. 'So what we don't want you to do is threaten his position.'

She was getting tired of his pedantic exposition.

'Look, I can't go back and I need somewhere to stay. I gave up my flat when I moved in with him.'

'I was getting to that. I think we'll go and see Julie. Move you in there for a time until we can set you up in your own place.'

'Who's Julie?'

'A friend. You'll like her.'

'I don't like sharing. Specially when the punters . . . I mean the clients come in. I've always had a place of my own.'

'This is a temporary measure until we can sort you out. Anyway, he may not have recognized you and you, for your part, are not absolutely certain he is a detective. Or if he is that he came from Cannon Row. Remember, my dear, police also have these urges.'

'They can usually get whatever they like as a freebie,' she said.

55

Goater had a white BMW to match his white clerical collar and drove her to a block of flats in Lancaster Gate. Frenchy was glad to see they were solid mansion flats built pre-war. There were two flats on each floor with front doors on opposite sides of the lift shaft. Julie's was on the second floor. Goater rang the doorbell.

After some moments he rang again.

'She might be out,' Frenchy said.

'There should be a porter somewhere.'

Frenchy turned the door handle. 'It's open.'

Goater frowned. They went in together.

'Someone's been having a barbecue,' she said.

The flat was dark. The smell was stronger as they went along a central passage.

Goater turned on lights. The living room was untidy. A couple of empty wine bottles stood on a low table. They went further up the passage. Goater opened a door. It was the main bedroom and the smell really hit them. It wasn't only the smell of grilling meat but something else too. Then Frenchy saw there was a figure on the bed.

'Oh, God!' she said.

Goater switched on the light and what they saw was very nasty indeed.

George Macrae opened the door of his house and switched on the lights. It had an empty feeling to it that he wasn't accustomed to nowadays. Frenchy was usually ready with a drink when he came home. He wandered into the kitchen then the sitting-room. Everything was neat and tidy. That was something else he had got used to. When he lived by himself he left the dishes and the tidying up for a once-a-week blitz. But he had to admit that a tidy house was a lot better than an untidy one.

He wondered where she was. Perhaps at the supermarket or at these new classes of hers. He felt ashamed that she had had to use her own money to cover expenses.

He poured himself a whisky and sat down in the sitting-room. There wasn't enough money to go round, that was the problem. There never had been.

His daughter Susan by his first marriage was still swanning around the world, last heard of in Australia. He had had to find money for her – and that had nearly wrecked his career.* Then there were the two kids by his second wife. They were growing up. There was money needed for them.

The cake wasn't very big but the slices were getting bigger.

He thought of the conversation he'd had with Les Wilson. If the Sheild Report went through as it was, Les was in for the chop. They'd been together a long time and it wasn't fair for a man to be pitched out of his job because the Government said they didn't need chief superintendents any longer. Yet it

Never Die in January (Pan Macmillan).

might even do Les a favour. They'd give him a golden handshake; he'd get his pension and if he did go into private security there was good money to be made. It was the growth industry of the nineties.

Macrae had never given a moment's serious thought to private security although he'd been asked a dozen times to leave the police and join this firm or that. He didn't fancy poking about in warehouses to see who'd nicked a case of Scotch, or spying on accident victims on behalf of their insurance companies to see whether they were as incapacitated as they alleged.

He didn't like that kind of work and never would. It was the Metropolitan Police or nothing, even if he went down the financial tubes.

Of course there were opportunities in the police to make a little extra and Macrae had known many officers who'd done just that. And he'd been offered cash in varying quantities to look the other way on many an occasion. He had frequently used violence on the villain so offering. It wasn't so much that his moral sense had been outraged; it was that the offers upset his touchy Highland dignity.

Another Scot, Macrae's ex-guv'nor, Chief Superintendent Bulloch, against whom there had never been the whiff of suspicion, used to call villains 'the filth'. He had used the term again just recently in the Rake. He was right. They *were* filth. And you didn't take money from filth.

What Macrae most liked was to put the filth

behind bars, but even that was becoming more problematical with the Crown Prosecution Service refusing to prosecute a high percentage of those arrested because it was too expensive.

Money . . . Money . . . Money . . .

The phone rang.

It would be Frenchy, he thought.

But the voice was that of Chief Superintendent Wilson.

'George?'

'Aye.'

'I've got one for you.'

Chapter Seven

No. 4 Sebastopol Mansions, London W.1. 9.38 p.m.
Weather: cold and clear.

The apartment comprised sitting-room, dining-room, main bedroom, two smaller bedrooms, two bathrooms, kitchen, larder. A police constable stood guard at the front door. Inside, there was a detective constable, a doctor, a team of three forensic officers, a photographer, a scene-of-crime officer – and Detective Superintendent George Macrae representing Area Major Incident Pool (8) of the Metropolitan Police. He had come through the front door like a large and threatening weather system.

'Where?' he said to several apprehensive faces.

'Main bedroom, sir.'

Macrae took out a handkerchief, held it to his nose and went in. A young doctor, working on the rota schedule, was packing away his gear. Macrae had not come across him before.

'She's dead all right,' the doctor said.

'Any ideas?'

'About what?'

Macrae stared at him. 'Is this your first?'

'It is. And I don't want another if they're all like this.'

'Any idea what happened? How she died?'

'I'm not going to guess. First thing they said to me, don't start guessing when the police ask you. Dead or alive. That's my function. And I say she's dead.'

'Well, that's lovely.'

'No more, no less.'

With heavy sarcasm Macrae said, 'Would it be possible for you to say if the pathologist has been contacted?'

'Quite possible. He's on his way. Good evening.'

Macrae followed him out of the room and again said to the enquiring faces, 'Anyone heard from Sergeant Silver?'

A voice at the door said, 'I'm here, guv'nor.'

'Where the hell were you?' Macrae gave release to his irritation.

'I had to go out.'

'Out?'

He managed to invest the word with a host of meanings ranging from suspicion to bewilderment, as though 'going out' was something performed in secret by degenerates.

Leo knew that as far as Macrae was concerned you were on duty twenty-four hours a day, seven days a week – and to hell with the new policing methods which postulated nine to five and as little overtime as possible.

To Macrae crime had no time limits, nor did policing. And it was for this reason – among others – that Silver worked for him so willingly. You only had to be near Macrae as he went up through his gears – as he was now – to get a charge. Gone was the boozy unfulfilled figure of the past weeks. Instead the big man dominated the apartment not only by his size but by the force of his personality. He hardly looked the same person.

'Right, laddie, let's see what we can see.'

The two of them went into the bedroom and shut the door.

'Lights,' Macrae said.

Leo switched on the bright centre light with his elbow. The woman's skin, garishly lit, looked like something in a museum case preserved in formaldehyde. But that was where the similarity ended. She was lying on her side on a king-size bed with a buttoned red satin headboard. In life she might have been attractive had she not been so painfully thin. Her hair was also thin and had lost its sheen and body. There had clearly been a struggle, for her skirt was hiked up and her long thin legs were visible. There was needle scarring on her right thigh and bruise marks. She was wearing her panties, and her bra was visible under a blouse. There were no obvious signs of sexual molestation.

Her ankles were bound with electric flex and more flex anchored her left arm to the side of the bed. Her right arm was unbound. Her mouth was stuffed with pink toilet paper and sealed with brown parcel tape.

Macrae went to the bedroom door. 'Who was here first?'

'DC Tompkins, sir,' a voice said.

'Where are you, Tompkins?'

'Sir.' A young detective constable in a check sports jacket came forward.

'I want you in here,' Macrae said.

'In there, sir?'

'What's the matter, laddie, you look green?'

'Smell, sir.'

'Have you never been to a barbecue?'

The police photographer laughed.

'What I want is her name, age and occupation.'

'We've got the porter, sir.'

Macrae noticed a man on crutches standing in the main doorway. 'Who's that gawping?'

'Neighbour, sir.'

'Well, tell him to fuck off.'

'Says he might be able to help, sir.'

'Oh. Well, tell him to go away quietly and we'll get to him.'

'And the porter, sir?'

'What are you, Tompkins? A probationer?'

'Yes, sir.'

'My God, you and the doctor. We've got the nursery school here tonight.'

There was a sycophantic murmur of laughter.

Macrae said, 'Just for now you tell me about her, Tompkins.'

Tompkins looked at his notebook and frowned. Macrae noted the shaking hands and remembered his own illegible notes when he was a probationer. 'Take a deep breath, laddie. OK? Right. Let's have it.'

'Time of arrival 8.14 p.m., sir. Woman's body on bed. Name Julia Maddox.' (He scowled at his handwriting.) 'Age unknown but the doctor guessed about thirty. Occupation unknown.'

'All right,' Macrae said. 'Line up the porter and the neighbour and any others who may have seen anything.'

He went back into the bedroom where Silver was making notes.

'Look on the floor, guv'nor.'

Partly hidden under the bed was what looked like a seventeenth-century bedwarmer, only smaller. It had two long handles which opened and closed concave metal discs.

'Has the room been photographed?' Macrae called from the doorway. When the photographer said it had he pulled out the contraption and placed it on a chair. 'What the hell is it?'

'I think it's for making *croque monsieur,*' Leo said.

'For making *what*?'

'Those French sandwiches, guv'nor.'

'You trying to be funny?'

'You put the filling between two slices, cut the bread to fit the shape of the discs, butter them on

64

the outside, fit them in, close the handles, and hold the thing over a gas flame. Makes the sandwich lovely and crisp on the outside and heats the filling at the same time.'

Macrae stared at him. 'Where did you learn that, laddie, at your uni-ver-sity?'

'Zoe makes them sometimes.'

'Does she call them crock whatever?'

'She calls them toasted sandwiches.'

'I wish she was my sergeant. Anyway . . . never mind that now. What I want to know is why did someone make a sandwich of Ms Maddox's left hand.'

Leo stared at the hand. It was yellow and black, the colour of a snake he had seen when he was on holiday in Namibia. 'S & M?' he said.

'With her underclothing on?' Macrae shouted to Tompkins. 'What do they cook with here? Electricity or gas?'

Tompkins appeared at the door. 'Gas, sir.'

'Whoever did this must have heated the thing in the kitchen, come into the bedroom, put her hand in it, burned her, gone back to the kitchen, heated it up . . . maybe three times or more. It takes a very special person.'

'But that wouldn't have killed her,' Leo said.

'No, but the mouthful of paper might've. The pathologist will tell us that. We'll leave this for the moment. Tompkins. Let's have the porter.'

The two detectives went into a spare bedroom, arranged a chair and a table, then the porter was brought in. He was about forty, small, thin, dark haired, with a foxy face. And he was nervous, licking his lips like a chameleon.

'Mr Takorides,' Macrae said, looking at Tompkins's notes. 'Greek?'

'Cypriot, sir.' His tongue zipped quickly along his lips.

'Always wanted to go to Cyprus but I never quite got there. All right, Mr Takorides, you reported the murder. Tell us about it.'

'Sir, my phone rings and—'

'Where's that?' Leo said.

'Around the corner. Alma Road.'

'All right, go on.'

'And a man, he says, there is a dead body in number four. I say you are making a joke. He say go and see. I come and see. I phone police.'

'What did this man sound like? Educated or not?'

'He sound like a man. I come from Cyprus. How I know whether he educated? He sound like Englishman.'

Leo said, 'Upper class? Lower class? What?'

Mr Takorides shrugged. 'How I can tell?'

Macrae said, 'Tell me about Miss Maddox – it is Miss, is it?'

'I don't know, sir.'

'Never mind, we'll check her out. How long has she been living here?'

'I don't know, sir.'

Macrae frowned. 'How long have you been the porter here?'

'Five years, sir.'

'Was she here when you came?'

'I don't know, sir.'

Zip . . . zip . . . went the tongue.

'Tompkins!'

'Sir?' The young officer stood in the doorway.

'Has Mr Takorides made any telephone calls since you brought him here?'

'Yes, sir. One, sir.'

Macrae turned to the porter. 'Who did you ring, laddie?'

Silence.

'All right, I'll tell you. You phoned the owners of the apartment block, didn't you?'

Silence.

'And you told them what had happened and they said don't tell the police anything. Isn't that so? By the way, what's your first name?'

'Hector.'

'Are you married, Hector?'

There was a pause as Takorides pondered this. Then he said, 'Yes, sir.'

'Kids?'

'Two, sir.'

'I've got three. I'm sure you want to see them again, Hector, and I don't only mean tonight. Because I'll tell you what's going to happen to you. Under the new Criminal Justice Act all that rubbish about the accused person having the right to silence has gone out the window and—'

'Accused?' Mr Takorides had gone paler than his normal sallow colour. 'Sir, I—'

'You interrupted me, Hector. Mustn't do that. What was I—? Oh, yes, the right to silence. Not a right any longer. Home Secretary says so – and about bloody time too. So, my wee Cypriot laddie, if you don't start to talk to me and answer my questions properly here's what I'm going to do: I'm going to arrest you for obstructing the police in the course of their duties and I'm going to have you prosecuted. The maximum sentence is six years and in cases where the police are obstructed in a murder investigation the court will hand down the maximum, you can bet on that.'

Mr Takorides looked stunned.

So did Leo.

He had never heard Macrae produce such a tissue of lies before. Six years! His usual method of interrogation was to depend on the ultimate sanction of violence. Was he mellowing with age?

'*Obstructum criminalis,*' Macrae said, menacingly. 'That's what it's called, Hector.'

Leo had to restrain himself from bursting into laughter.

'But Mr Volker sack me,' said the porter. 'I lose my job.'

'You have to make up your mind,' Macrae said, tapping the table with his fingers. 'Mr Volker or me.'

Mr Takorides looked down at his hands.

'Did you make a call to the owners?'

'Yes, sir, I phone Mr Volker. And he say I must speak about nothing. I must say I know nothing.'

'But you do know something, don't you, Hector? Indeed you may know everything. You may even have done it.'

'Sir, I swear you on my father's grave I not do it.'

'That's a terrific oath, Hector, and I believe you. I don't think a man would swear on his father's grave lightly.' He turned to Silver. 'Do you?'

'No, guv'nor. Not lightly.'

Macrae said, 'We believe you. We think you didn't do it. But we have to be *sure*. Let me explain something to you. We don't know when she died. It may have been yesterday or the day before that or last week. There's no central heating in the bedroom and in this cold weather . . . well, I don't have to explain, do I. So I want you to think very carefully what you were doing these past few days. Every day. Because we're going to check up on you. Do you follow me, Hector?'

'Yes, sir.'

'Right. Now, what did Miss Maddox do for a living?'

'I do not know, sir.'

'Tompkins!'

'Sir.'

'I want you to take Mr Takorides into the sitting-room and stay with him. Keep your pencil and notebook handy. He is going to do some memory work for us. He's going to tell you what he's been doing in the past few days, say back to last Friday. And you're going to take it down, this time legibly. Oh, and no more phone calls.'

Tompkins led Takorides into the drawing-room.

Macrae said, 'He's lying. He knows what that voice was like. I never met a porter in my life who wasn't a snob, even if he does come from Cyprus. I'll have a word with Mr Volker, I think.'

'We could charge him too,' Leo said.

'What for?'

'*Obstructum criminalis?*'

Macrae looked at him blank-faced. 'Didn't they teach you that?'

'I didn't take law, guv'nor. But since we're on words Zoe's just been to Edinburgh and when she came back she called me a cannegotian. Said I should ask you what it meant.'

Macrae smiled. It was rare enough to be significant. 'That's what my mother used to call me when I was a child if I was messing about with my food. God, I haven't heard it for years. I think it came from the rough and vulgar people who used to live in the Cannongate in Edinburgh so it fits you perfectly.'

'Sir,' a voice said. 'Pathologist's here.'

They went into the bedroom. 'Oh, it's you, Macrae. I might have known. They save up all the horrors for you, don't they?'

Dr Ramsden was dressed in worn corduroys and

filthy tennis shoes. He was middle aged, grey faced, his dark hair shot through with white.

'I'd just got to bed,' he said. 'Dreaming of something nice. Sunlit uplands. Green grass. Daisies. Now this.'

The three men stood looking down at the wax-work figure. Ramsden gave a deep sigh. 'What a way to make a living.'

Chapter Eight

Macrae and Silver went across the lobby to the opposite apartment. The man on crutches met them at the door.

'I will not be told to fuck off!' he said to Macrae. 'Not by you! Not by anybody!'

They did not react, instead Macrae moved past him into his drawing-room. He hobbled in after them. He was tall and craggy and in his sixties. 'D'you hear what I said!' It was almost a shout. 'D'you know who I am?'

Macrae looked at his notes. 'Mr Baldwin.'

'No, I am *not* Mr Baldwin. I am Sir Marcus Baldwin. Do you know what that means?'

Macrae ignored him for a moment and looked around. The walls were covered in shields and swords and ancient weapons of war. 'No, sir, I don't.'

'Don't you read the newspapers, man? I've just come back from the South Pole. The oldest person to walk there. Carried all my own food. Don't you watch television? Didn't you see me interviewed?'

'Must have missed it.'

Sir Marcus was angry. 'Good God, and you're supposed to be detectives! Don't they teach you to keep abreast of the news?'

'No, sir.'

'Doesn't the name Baldwin mean anything to you? King Baldwin?'

'King Baldwin?' Macrae said.

'Yes, yes, King Baldwin of Jerusalem, Count of Edessa. The First Crusade, man. Surely you've heard of the Crusades?'

'Yes, sir.'

'Well, I'm a direct descendant. Who are you descended from?'

'We'll have to leave family trees and the Crusades if you don't mind, sir,' Macrae said. 'I've got something rather more important on my hands. One of my officers said you might be able to help our investigation into the death of Miss Maddox.'

'Death?' He laughed shortly. 'D'you think I'm a child? It was murder, wasn't it? Of course it was!'

'We don't know that yet. We don't know anything very much. We've only just started our investigations. You wouldn't want us to jump to conclusions.'

'Oh, Christ, I've got to sit down.' He waved them to chairs and fell into one himself. 'Frostbite.' He indicated his heavily bandaged feet. 'Can't tell you how bloody painful it is when they come and take the dressings off. You ever seen frostbite?'

'I don't think so,' Macrae said.

73

'You'd remember if you had. Black. That's what happens. Skin goes all black and you have to cut it away with scissors. Horrible bloody business. They still don't know if they'll save my toes. Are you sure you didn't read about me? I was in the papers for weeks.'

'No, sir, we didn't,' Leo said.

'Bloody amazing. Thought everyone would've. You will when the book's finished. Oh, that'll be quite something. Oldest man ever to get to the Pole. And walking! Not like some of these other swines. Freaks, I call 'em. There was a Frenchman who was motorcycling to the Pole. Motorcycling! Can you believe it! Had a back-up team. Flew in from Punta Arenas with a team of mechanics and doctors and food specialists. I mean the whole thing was a bloody stunt. The swine are everywhere. Not only French. Japanese. Austrian. You name it. And doing bloody silly things. Climbing up Everest backwards. Swimming the Channel with one hand tied behind their backs. Roller skating on the Moon.'

'On the Moon?' Leo said.

'Well, you know what I mean. They will be soon enough.'

'Can we get back to Miss Maddox?'

'Yes, yes. Mustn't let me get carried away. Exploration's my hobby. Don't do it for the money either. Not like some. Can't you just imagine it? I mean when the bills come in and the fellow says to the wife: "God, look at all these bills, Daphne, I'll have to go and explore something." ' He bent over, laughing, then grabbed his leg and said, 'Oooh Christ! That was a naughty one.'

'Tell us about Miss Maddox,' Macrae said. 'How long have you known her?'

'Right. Miss Maddox. Known her? Well, she came here about two years ago. I've been here since God knows when. Can't really say I *know* her. Seen her in the lift of course. Good morning. That sort of thing. But I'm away a lot. South Pole. North Pole. The Amazon. The Empty Quarter . . .'

'Did she have many visitors?' Leo cut in.

'Well, yes, I suppose she did. Miss Maddox liked the boys. Bit thin for my taste. Always reminded me of a cobra. Tall. Willowy.'

'Lots of men friends?'

'Rather. Used to come up in the lift with them often enough.'

'What sort?'

'What d'you mean?'

'Well, were they—?'

'He means gents or yobs,' Macrae said, briskly.

'How the bloody hell can you tell these days?'

'Were they all different? I mean did you recognize any as coming frequently?'

'There was one chap. He delivered pizzas. He used to come often. I thought to myself, *she* must eat a lot of rubbish. But that was about all. Except for today.'

'Tell us about today.'

'I was having my feet done. They sent a nurse along at first but she hurt like the blazes and I said no you bloody don't I've had Freddy for years and I'll have him rather than her. And they said, "Who's Freddy?" and I said, "He's my chiropodist." Saved my feet once before when I came back from Brazil. Knows a bloody sight more about feet than a hospital nurse.'

Macrae said, 'Go on.'

'Anyway, he was just leaving and he said to me, "Something's going on opposite." Those aren't his exact words, of course. And I said, "What's going on, Freddy?" And he said, "She's seeing a priest." And I said, "That's a surprise," or words to that effect.'

'And?' Macrae said.

'And what?'

'Go on.'

'That's enough, isn't it? The woman's murdered. A priest is seen coming out of her door. Find the priest. Good God, man, do I even have to do your bloody job for you!'

They spent another twenty minutes with Sir Marcus and learned a great deal about ice walls, moraines, crevasses, polar tents, eating out of tubes and urinating at minus 40 degrees; but not a great deal more about the mutilated body in the apartment opposite.

'Go and talk to Freddy,' Sir Marcus said. 'Tell him I said so. Bloody brilliant. Especially with dorsal bunions.'

'What's a dorsal bunion, guv'nor?' Leo asked as they walked back to Julie Maddox's flat.

'I thought you were supposed to be educated,' Macrae said. 'Tompkins!'

'Sir!' The probationer appeared at the sitting-room door.

'Well?'

'He's remembering bits and pieces, sir, but there are a lot of gaps.'

'He fills in the gaps or you book him,' Macrae said.

Tompkins looked apprehensive. 'What charge, sir?'

'*Obstructum criminalis*,' Leo said, gravely.

Macrae nodded. 'That'll do to start with.'

Tompkins said, 'Sir, he's been crying.'

'Well, blow his nose for him. Tell him I want the names of all the pizza places around here. And I want to know about the men who came to see Miss Maddox. Tell him he'd better bloody start remembering.'

Dr Ramsden was finishing his preliminary examination when they went back to the bedroom. The smell hit them again, worse than the first time.

'What can you tell us, doc?'

'Nothing much at this stage.'

'Anything would be a help.'

'The cause of death is probably suffocation. I've had the tape off her mouth and the paper has gone down a long way. Enough to cut off the air supply.

Probably happened when she was struggling.' He indicated the rumpled skirt and blankets.

'S & M?'

'Never. You dress up for that, and anyway injuries and deaths usually happen by accident. Don't forget you're supposed to be enjoying yourself. She certainly didn't. And her bra and pants are on. Sexual organs undamaged but I'd say she had had a hell of a sex life. I've found dozens of hairs on the duvet and the pillows. From what I can tell here they're mostly different. I'll have a look at them more closely.'

He closed his bag.

'Is that it?' Macrae said.

'For the moment.'

'Doc, when you do the PM would you have a good look at the stomach contents?'

'Anything particular?'

'Pizzas.'

At the door Ramsden said, 'She was on drugs, as you probably saw. My guess would be heroin. But I'll let you know about that too.'

Everything comes to an end, he had said.

You want someone else, she had said.

That's not true.

It is . . . don't lie to me!

They were in his room. They had made love and then had started to argue. She had got dressed because she could not argue naked. It hadn't bothered him.

OK, what if I said it was true, that I did want someone else?

It is, then, isn't it?

This is your scenario, remember. The problem is you want me to say yes and you want me to say no. What you can't handle is the simple fact that I might not want this to go on.

Nonsense, she had said.

You can't handle it because it's too humiliating. If there was someone else you'd be able to salvage something. You'd have something to vent your anger on. You can always fall back on the old cliché, he left me for another woman. But he just left me. See how bad it sounds?

Are you?

What?

Just walking out?

Isn't that what I said?

Tell me the truth, she had said.

You want the truth? Really?

Of course I do.

I thought you wanted me to lie.

You shit, she had said. You think you're so fucking smart.

Yes, I do. And I am. But it doesn't change anything. You've always been attracted to the wrong men. I'm wrong for you. But you like being trampled on. Some women are like that. Look, I'm not saying we didn't have some fun—

You bastard!

What now?

Don't patronize me.

*You wanted the truth but when you hear it you don't
like it.*

*For God's sake, David, it's all booked. Everything's
arranged. Paid for.*

I'm not going. Get used to it.

But we've talked and planned and lived for it.

You have. You never bloody stopped.

Pause.

*How much more humiliation could she take? Was
there a limit?*

Please, she had said. Please . . .

Forget it.

*The phone rang and he answered it. You must have
the wrong number, he had said. But the way he had
cupped the mouthpiece and looked at her, she knew.*

*Later she had found out he had been lying. There
had been someone else. But he had chosen to go for the
big H. The big humiliation. The ball breaker.*

Leo reached home around one in the morning. Zoe
was asleep. There was a note for him which read:
*Roses are red/Violets are blue/Your food's in the oven/
And I love you Leopold Silver.*

He screwed up the paper and threw it in the
basket in the kitchen. He looked in the oven. There
was a small fisherman's pie from Sainsbury. A note

on the oven door said: Heat for fifteen minutes. There's ice cream in the freezer.

He couldn't face food. He poured himself a whisky instead and wandered over to the windows overlooking the street. He saw his face reflected in the window. It looked tired and drawn. That was the image he had expected to see, but then it changed and he was seeing Laura in the hospital bed, her hair spread out on the pillow. She had looked so clean, so innocent, so different from his own world where women had toilet paper stuffed down their throats and their hands burnt beyond recognition.

And he had nearly turned Laura into something from that side of his life. The bump on the head had just been a bump. But if he'd been going slightly faster the impact would have been harder, the blow to her head greater. He could hardly bear to think about it.

Macrae lay in his bed very conscious that he was alone. He had become so used to Frenchy being there that it was like suddenly missing an arm or a leg.

There had been a message on the answer machine when he came back in the early hours.

'Listen, love, I've gone to see Mum. Will stay with her for a few days. There's sausages and bacon in the fridge. A bit of liver too. I hope you miss me.'

He did.

He'd better get a grip on himself. This was no good. Les Wilson was right. If Scales found he was living with a known prostitute he'd have him off the Force in a minute.

For the third or fourth time he wondered what working in private security would be like. There was one good thing about it, the bosses couldn't give a stuff who you were living with.

Of course if he married her . . . well, that would change things.

But he cringed at the thought of a third marriage. So far two failed marriages had cost him a fortune.

Then, abruptly, a chastening thought entered his mind: what if he asked her and she said no?

Chapter Nine

'Right, ladies, can we make a start?' she said. 'Let's see, how many are there today? Two – four – six – eight – ten – eleven. Not marvellous. Maybe it's the cold. Brrrr . . .' she rubbed her hands. 'It's freezing in here. I know the Church is supposed to be skint, but this is ridiculous.'

'We tried turning up the heating but it's stuck,' Frenchy said.

'It's not going to help just standing here. Sooner we start, sooner we'll warm up.'

The eleven women, mostly young, were dressed in white tops and white baggy trousers and were barefooted. Frenchy's toes were blue. So were the mats which covered a quarter of the floor space, so was the air which haloed the ceiling lights of the church hall.

'OK,' the instructor said. 'We've got to be careful we don't pull any muscles. By the way, any of you read that story in the papers? The lady who was tied up and burned? Well, it's not going to happen to us. That's what we're here to learn to avoid. Right?'

'Right!' they chorused.

'My mother tried to bring me up to be what she called a nice girl, but we're not going to be nice girls, are we?'

'No!' they chorused.

'We're going to fight back. We're going to crock 'em. Right?'

'Right!' There was real aggression now.

'OK. Brilliant. I'm sure you've been told the history of aikido but I just want to remind you of the most important thing of all. Anybody?'

'The Way,' someone said.

'The Way. Right. I can teach you how to throw your partners through the wall but it's not really going to help unless you discover the Way. I can't find it for you. I can only show you where to look.' She tapped her small and athletic breast. 'Here. This is where you look. Inside yourself. If we had more time and it wasn't so fucking cold I'd tell you about Morihei Ueshiba and Takeda Sokaku—'

'We've learned about them,' a voice said.

'Let's get to it, then. Technique – technique – technique— First we're going to do some falling. That'll warm you up. Then we'll do an elbow lock. OK? Right then. We know we've got to learn to fall safely. So we fall in a rotating movement called a roll-out. Please assume the squatting position . . .'

An hour later Frenchy let herself into Goater's apartment near the Park. She was warm, indeed perspiring into her thick tracksuit.

'I'm going to take a shower, OK?'

Goater was seated in front of his computer, tapping at the keyboard and speaking on the phone. He waved to her and said into the phone. 'You had Dolores last time. Yes . . . Yes . . . I'm positive. Of course, if you want to. Dust pan and brush. Apron. You realize it'll cost more? Fine. I'll tell her. No . . . no . . . don't say your name. You're just a number. Safer that way.'

Frenchy went into her bedroom, stripped off and walked to the bathroom. The shower was powerful and the hot water turned her skin pink. She put on needle jets of ice cold which made her gasp. She came out, towelled herself briskly. Her body felt supple and alive. When she looked round, Goater was standing by the washbasin.

Instinctively she covered her damaged breast. 'You like to look?'

'Only when the view is exceptional. You must remember I live in a world of wonderful views. But you are exceptional. You want to play a little?'

'Play? You mean chains and leather?'

'Not at all. I mean a little light lunch: smoked salmon. Dom Perignon. A joint or two. You know . . .'

'You buying my time?'

'I just thought—'

'Well, don't think.'

'My dear, there are some people in my profession who'd break your arms and legs if you acted this way with them.'

'And there are some in my profession who have friends in other professions.'

'Mr Macrae?'

'The same.'

'I don't know what you see – never mind. We've been down that road before.'

'Listen, I'm grateful for the bed et cetera but I'm going to Mum's. I'll stay there for a bit.'

'I'll be sad to see you go in one way, but maybe it's for the best. Just remember to keep your mouth shut.'

'You don't have to tell me. But ... what if the punter coming out of the other flat *did* see us?'

'Forget it. Even if he did it could only have been our coats and hats. You were wearing your woolly hat, weren't you?'

'A small black man with a clerical collar? And a tall white woman? Be your age! Why d'you wear that silly collar anyway?'

'I was going into the Church once. It's a kind of talisman.'

'A what?'

He didn't reply but she could see he was troubled.

'And I don't know what I'm going to say to Mr Macrae,' she said.

'About what?'

'About anything.' She picked up a magazine from one of the Sunday papers and flicked through it until she found the astrological information. 'Capricorn,' she said. 'That's what Mr Macrae is.' She read out.

' "Prediction requires the capacity to imagine the events described; but at times during which what is taking place is not change in the conventional sense . . ." ' she began to falter. 'D'you understand that?'

Goater shook his head. 'Do you?'

'I know what I'll do. I'll ask Mum for a horoscope.'

'Got a minute, George?'

Macrae was at his desk gathering together cigars and matches. Les Wilson was standing at the door of his office.

'I'm on my way, Les. The pathologist says she suffocated. And *was* on heroin.'

'Oh.' Wilson didn't sound too interested in the murder of which he was in charge. 'Listen, George, what I wanted to ask you was have you had any dealings with a DCI called Michaelson? He was at the Yard until a couple of years ago. Ex-Murder Squad.'

'Don't think so, why?'

'It's just that he's head of security at International Foods.'

'Who are they?'

'The big drinks and food company. They own a string of liquor shops too.'

'Les, I know damn all about private security.'

'Just thought I'd ask. You seen the chiropodist bloke yet?'

'That's where I'm going now.'

'Keep me posted.'

Macrae grunted. Wilson, who liked charts and graphs and different coloured stickers – colour coding drove Macrae mad – hadn't been at the sharp end of a murder investigation for years and suddenly Macrae realized that if his rank was made redundant as the Sheild Report was advocating, his loss would hardly cause a ripple. Another thought crossed his mind: without Wilson there would be no buffer between himself and Scales and that was likely to turn the aggro up a few notches.

Wilson went off down the corridor to his own office and Macrae reached for his overcoat. There was a soft knock on his door. A large man in his early thirties with heavy sideburns said, 'Could I have a word, sir?'

'Who are you?'

'DS Lightly, sir.'

'What about?'

'I wanted to get your advice about something.'

'It'll have to wait. I'm on my way.'

'Anything you say, sir.'

Macrae looked up. There had been an inflection in the voice that didn't match the sense of what he had said. But the face was blank and the eyes were sincere and Macrae was suddenly made to feel guilty. He had been down on the younger officers of late. Usually he had a good relationship with them.

'Let's have a drink later,' he said.

He went out of the building. The late autumn

sunshine was striking the Thames. Over recent years the buildings along the river had been cleaned and the stonework gleamed whitely. It contrasted dramatically with the blue of the sky and the dark burnished water.

Silver, who was waiting with the car, said, 'Not bad, guv'nor.' He indicated the sky and the city.

'You're getting poetic,' Macrae said. 'Must be your education.'

'Where to?'

'Paddington. Just where I'd expect a chiropodist to be.'

The rooms were above a kebab house and the smell of grilling lamb was strong on the staircase. The stair carpet was showing its age and the wall was marked near the light switch by a thousand greasy fingers. A notice on a door on the first floor landing said, 'F. Coker, M.S.S.Ch., M.B., Ch.A. Disorders of the Foot, Surgery & Domiciliary Visits. By Appointment Only.' This last had had a line put through it.

Macrae banged at the door and, after a moment, it was opened by an elderly man, thin and almost bald, with the largest bags under his eyes Leo had ever seen. He was dressed in a white coat, brown trousers and carpet slippers.

'Do you have an appointment?' He glanced down at their feet.

'Do we need one?'

'No, I don't suppose you do.'

'Mr Frederick Coker?'

'The same.'

Macrae identified them. 'Oh, yes, Sir Marcus said you'd be round.'

He led them through the small waiting-room into an adjoining room which contained a desk and a couple of chairs. Macrae and Silver sat down on the chairs but Mr Coker perched on a low stool as though about to give them a treatment. The walls were covered in framed diplomas and large yellowing illustrations of feet. Leo looked briefly at them before sitting down, which was a mistake. Mr Coker instantly leapt up and said, 'You'd be interested in feet, being policemen. See that there?'

He pointed to one of the illustrations and Leo looked more closely. He wished he hadn't. Coker was indicating what had at first looked like a shadow between the first and second toes. 'Athlete's foot. Like grey mould sometimes. The sort you'd see on bread. Gets so bad you can peel it off.'

Leo felt his own feet begin to itch. He looked away but found himself staring at what might have been an electric nail file. It resembled an antiquated dentist's drill and stood beside a table covered with creams, powders, cotton wool, orange sponges and a kidney-shaped dish containing a collection of razor-blade holders.

'Veruccas.' Coker was pointing to another illustration. 'And ingrowing nails. If you look carefully . . . just there . . . you can see the pus.'

'Mr Coker,' Macrae said.

'Take care of your feet, I always say, and the rest will follow. See that?' He tapped an illustration. 'You wouldn't think corns grew *under* nails, now would you? But they do, the little beggars. Then what you've got to do is drill—'

'Mr Coker!'

'. . . a hole and lift them out.'

'Mr Coker! Can we get to your last visit to Sir Marcus Baldwin.' Leo was desperate to get away from feet.

'You should have seen *his* feet when he came back from South America. You'd never believe the fungal growth. All red and yellow. Now the toes are black with frostbite and—'

'For pity's sake, shut up about toes and feet,' Macrae said. 'You're making me feel ill.'

'They do that to some people,' Mr Coker said. 'Can't think why.'

'Tell us what happened.'

'Well, I'd finished my treatment and Sir Marcus had given me his cheque and he said, "Freddy, you know the way to the door" – he always calls me Freddy – and I said, "Like the back of my foot." A little joke we have. You know, about feet. All feet on deck . . . the foot that rocks the cradle . . . that sort of thing.' He made a soft, lugubrious sound which Leo took to be a laugh.

Macrae gave signs of an imminent eruption and Leo said hastily, 'What did you see at the door?'

'Pair of black half-brogues and a pair of purple slingbacks. Could have been mauve or blue. The light wasn't too good.'

Macrae scowled at him. 'Who the hell were in the shoes?'

'A man and a woman.'

'Go on. What else were they wearing.'

'I didn't really look at the rest of their clothing. It doesn't interest me, you see.'

'Their faces then!'

'Faces don't interest me either. But their feet. Oh, yes. Expensive shoes on the man, Church's most like, so he's all right. But if the lady isn't careful those stiletto heels are going to give her arch trouble, to say nothing of corns and bunions.'

'But you told Sir Marcus you'd seen a priest.'

'Oh, yes, so I did. It was the collar. I saw the collar.'

'Go on.'

'And I said to Sir Marcus, "Hello, something's going on opposite." And he said, "What?" And I said, "Search me, but she's seeing a priest." '

'And that's all?'

'I'm rather afraid it is.'

Chapter Ten

Leo reached the hospital in the late afternoon. He had phoned three times during the day but had been transferred twice to the incorrect ward and the third time had been cut off. Macrae had sat impatiently in the car while this was going on and then had said, 'What the hell's the matter with you? Have you got a bit on the side?'

So it was nearly five o'clock when Leo got to Fulham General.

'Who?' the receptionist said. She was an Afro-Caribbean lady of ample proportions who wore half-glasses on a cord.

'Parkes. Laura Parkes.'

'Parkes . . .' She began to punch a keyboard.

'She was due out today,' Leo said. 'Smallish. Blonde.'

The woman stared at him over the half-moons.

'Are you the hos-ban'?'

Leo began to speak but she fixed him with a ferocious glance and silenced him with a wave of her hand. 'You should be ashamed of yourself. Ashamed.

That woman sat there. Right there . . .' She pointed at a bench in the foyer. 'She sat there for an hour, maybe two. Waiting and waiting. You men are all alike; you wants your cake but you wants to eat it all up as well.'

'I'm not her husband. I hardly even—'

'Companion . . . partner . . . why you splittin' hairs? You left her, that's what I'm saying. You should be ashamed.'

Leo got back into his car feeling tired, irritated and guilty. He looked at the time. If he went to Putney in the rush-hour traffic he'd be late home. But he was often late home; it was that sort of job.

He went to Putney.

Her car was still where he'd left it. The dent was already showing faint signs of rust on the bare metal. It would have to be beaten out and resprayed. But whatever it cost, he'd pay.

He rang the bell and waited. Her flat was on the ground floor of a house that had been split into several flats. When she opened the door he said, 'Hi.'

She paused and said, 'Hello.' It was formal, unwelcoming, and she made no effort to ask him in. She was dressed in a long cheese-cloth dress. Round her neck were several strands of beads, some wooden, some bright coloured glass. She was wearing several copper bracelets on her arms and a single gold chain round one of her ankles. She was barefooted. Her hair was back in the pony tail he remembered and she wore a headband.

At first he thought: ethnic.

But later he was to realize she was a kind of reincarnation of the hippies of the sixties and seventies.

'Look, I'm sorry,' he said.

'What for?'

'For not picking you up and bringing you here.'

'Oh, that.'

She made it sound as though nothing could have been further from her mind.

'I said I would.'

'Yes, I remember.'

He told her about his difficulty in phoning.

She suddenly smiled her infectious smile. 'Poor Leo. Come on in.'

He followed her into her sitting-room, or into the room he imagined was her sitting-room, although it could have been a temple for worshippers of a religion with which he was not familiar.

The walls were black with a gold pattern. There were no conventional chairs but the floor was strewn with large Indian cushions. On the walls he saw brightly painted fish carved from wood, several nose flutes, a lute-like instrument, Pan pipes, demon masks and in one corner a couple of Tibetan prayer wheels. The air was drenched with the smell of incense and, from a couple of hidden speakers, came the soft whine of a sitar.

'Wow,' he said.

'You like it?'

'It's fantastic.'

'That's what it's meant to be. Have you read a book called *A Rebours*?'

'I know of it,' he lied.

'The central figure created a whole exotic world in his house. Different rooms for different moods. Fantastic and phantasmagoric. I can't afford that so I just did one. Would you like some tea?'

She came back with a teapot and two Chinese cups and they sipped jasmine tea.

'Nice,' he said. 'I like those, too.' He pointed to the wall ornaments.

'You're Jewish, aren't you?'

'Yes.'

'Jews care about beautiful things.'

He thought of his parents' apartment. It wasn't precisely bulging with *objets d'art*. Nor was his own flat, for that matter. Still . . . that didn't mean he wasn't able to appreciate beauty.

'They're not really beautiful in an artistic sense, but they have a functional beauty,' she said. 'Anyway I love collecting. What have you been doing today, Leo?'

'Look, there's something I should tell you.'

'That sounds ominous.'

'Not really. It's just that I'm a detective.'

She smiled. 'A real one?'

'A real one. In London.'

'Why didn't you say so at the time of the accident?'

'I . . . well . . . it's complicated. We were . . . my guv'nor and I—'

'Your what?'

'Guv'nor. That's what we call our senior officers. I mean the ones we work with. He's Detective Superintendent Macrae. He's the best. At thief-taking, that is. I mean catching criminals. I didn't tell you then because we were on a job when we had the accident. Under cover.'

'That sounds exciting?'

'It can be.'

'I've seen movies about undercover detectives,' she said.

'Yes, well, you don't want to believe everything you see on the box.'

She poured him more tea.

'Leo . . . detectives find people, don't they?'

'You mean missing people?'

'Yes. Trace them? Isn't there a missing persons bureau or something?'

'That's in America. There isn't really any centralized department in Britain. Each provincial force does it their way, so to speak. We've got a computer file for London. Why?'

'I just wondered. You see, my sister, Samantha . . .' She dried up.

'Is she missing?'

'No, someone else. But she . . . Oh, forget it.'

'No, no, tell me. If I can be of any help I'll try.'

'I couldn't ask you to do something like that

unless I told you some of the background and that's really dirty washing. Dirty family washing.'

'You must decide, but in my job we deal in dirty family washing twenty-four hours a day.'

'It's something that happened quite a long time ago . . . And . . . oh, I can't . . . But, hey, wait a sec. If Sam would talk to you, would that—?'

'Sure. Why not? I'd be glad to help.'

'Let me ask her. She probably won't but I could try. She's . . . well, she's all I've got. And I'm all she's got. And I worry about her. Have you any brothers or sisters?'

'A sister.'

'Then you'll know what I mean.'

Leo thought of Ruth. His relationship with her wasn't quite the same thing but he needn't go into that.

'Could I ring you after I've talked to her? Perhaps make a time for you to meet her?'

'Sure.' He rose. 'I'd better get going.' He took out his notebook, wrote down his rank and full name and gave her the page.

'A sergeant. I'm impressed.'

'Don't be.'

'What do you investigate?'

'Violent crime. This is the number for the station. If I'm not there leave a message.'

She saw him to the door. They shook hands formally. As he was leaving she said, 'Are you married, Leo?'

He paused fractionally. 'No,' he said.

At the car he turned to raise his hand but she'd gone and the door was closed.

'Sex and drugs,' Scales said. 'It's the same everywhere.'

He had walked into Macrae's room in early evening without knocking – something that infuriated Macrae – and had almost caught him reaching into his bottom drawer for the bottle of Famous Grouse which nestled there.

Scales was in his shirt-sleeves and his thin hair, combed sideways over his skull, was in need of resetting. It was an article of faith held by many at Cannon Row that every time he went to the men's room he took with him an aerosol can of Elnett hairspray.

'That's the thinking behind my crackdown on prostitution, George. Weed out the prostitutes and you remove the reason for a lot of drug dealing.'

Macrae lit a cigar. He didn't really feel like one but it was a small show of independence. 'There's no evidence yet that she was a prostitute,' he said.

'Course she was.'

The cigar smoke reached Scales and he clicked his ballpoint pen irritably.

'Drugs, aye, but we've still got to have evidence about prostitution.'

'Don't split hairs. You work on Taki-whatever his

name is. He'll break. We know that most tarts are on drugs these days. That's why a lot of them become tarts in the first place. To pay for the habit.' Click . . . click . . . went the pen.

Macrae felt his heart, after a spell of beating regularly, start to go *thump . . . thump*. Pause, *thump . . . thump*. Pause.

Scales said, 'When I was a kid my mother used to bring me up to town from Southsea and we could walk all round the West End without seeing a tart or a beggar. Beggars! In England! It's the sort of thing you expected to see in . . . well, not here anyway. Up the Strand at night they're sleeping in every shop doorway. Christ!'

Macrae pulled at his cigar, annoyed that he secretly agreed with Scales.

Scales said, 'Policemen have always had a soft spot for tarts. You only have to see what they're like when they book them or take them to court. Act more like brothers than police officers.'

'You've got to be sorry for some of them,' Macrae said. 'Their lives are a shambles. A lot have kids and it's the only way they can make their bread.'

'That's sentimental twaddle and I'm surprised to hear it coming from you. Who makes their lives a shambles?'

'Men.'

'You mean they were all nice girls once?'

'Aye. Stands to reason they must have been once.'

'I blame the people who mix with them,' Scales said. 'God, it makes me shudder just to think—'

There was a knock on the door. DS Lightly put his head round.

'Oh, sorry, sir,' he said to Scales. 'I didn't see—'

'That's all right. I'm on my way. George, keep me posted.'

Macrae glowered at his retreating back then said, 'Yes?'

'Sir, this morning you said we'd have a drink.'

'Oh, yes.' He looked down at the mass of papers on his desk. The police computers were supposed to have put an end to paperwork; instead it had quadrupled in the last few years. Macrae hated it with a deep and bitter hatred.

'All right, Lightly, but it'll have to be a quick one.'

The Red Lion was full of homeward-bound commuters wanting a couple of fast ones before the journey. The air was thick with smoke and loud with conversation. Just the sort of place Macrae liked.

'What'll you have, sir?'

He was about to order his usual, a shot of whisky and a pint of ale, but remembered who was buying and said, 'Pint of heavy.'

He watched Lightly go to the bar. It was two deep but he used his big shoulders to heave bodies aside. Heads turned angrily, but the expression on his face, the dark sideburns, the heavy Zapata moustache and the big frame, made them turn away. He came back with the drinks.

'Cheers, sir,' he said.

'Slainté.'

There was a momentary pause. Macrae had been in similar situations with junior officers before, men wanting advice because they had got into debt or were having problems with their families. Though why, with Macrae's own dismal track record in these departments, they came to him he was never sure.

'How are things going?' he said to get the ball rolling.

'Pretty good, thank you, sir.'

He seemed, to Macrae's surprise, to be quite relaxed.

'Right, what can I do for you?'

It was as though Lightly had not heard the question. He drank, wiped his moustache, and said, 'The station's been pretty disgusting the past few days.'

'You mean the dossers?'

'Yeah. And the tarts. We've pulled in more than ever before. Mr Scales is pleased.'

'They'll all be back on the streets as soon as they've paid their fines. Are you on it?'

'Yes, sir.'

Macrae looked at his watch.

'Am I keeping you, sir?' Lightly was concerned.

'I've got a hell of a lot on my plate at the moment and—'

'The case of the barbecued sandwich?' Lightly sniggered. 'That's what the lads are calling it.'

'Let's get to the point.'

'Right, sir. What I wanted to talk to you about was my prospects.'

'What the hell's that supposed to mean? In the force? In bed? What?'

'Bed's all right, sir, no problems there.' A macho note had crept into his voice.

'Well, that's a load off my mind.'

'No, in the police, sir. I'm thirty-two and I'm still a sergeant. I could earn twice what I make in private security.'

'Christ, everyone's talking about private security these days. Why don't you go into it, then?'

'Don't fancy it. I like being a copper. It's just that I have this ambitious streak.'

'That's no bad thing, laddie. Otherwise what's the point?'

'That's what I think, sir. Trouble is I can't seem to get any further up the ladder. I can't make inspector.'

'You know the route. Examinations. Selection boards.'

'The examinations are all right. I've passed those. It's the selection boards that I can't seem to convince. I've been up twice. I think they're against me.'

'If you want my advice, try a third time.'

'That's what I think, sir.'

'If you're failed again maybe you should think of transferring to another force outside London. The Surrey Police or Thames Valley. London's the toughest.'

'Trouble is I don't want to leave the Met.'

Macrae was becoming impatient. 'You don't sound as if you've thought this through, Lightly. You've got to consider alternatives.'

Lightly did not respond. Instead he looked at his ale for a long moment. 'Another drink, sir?'

'No, I must go. You've heard what I think. I don't believe there's anything more I can do.'

'Oh, but there is, sir.' Now the tone was sincere. 'The selection board meets next month. A word from you, sir . . .'

'Am I hearing right?'

'You could swing it, sir. Everyone respects your opinion.'

Macrae rose. 'I'm going to pretend I haven't had this talk. I think you should do the same. If I hear one more word I'm going to put the boot in.'

Lightly stood up and faced him. The two men were of a height. Lightly smiled. 'I had to have a try, sir. Everyone's got to do the best for themselves.'

'Don't say another word.'

'OK, sir. Give Frenchy my regards, sir.'

Macrae, who had begun to turn away, swung back. 'What was that?'

'Frenchy, sir. Very good-looking woman, if I may say so. I saw her the other night at the London Towers. Quite like old times. Give her my regards, sir. Oh . . . you needn't worry, sir. I never said a thing to Mr Scales. Not me. I'm not like that.'

Before Macrae could open his mouth Lightly was pushing through the crowd and had disappeared into the street.

Lysander Goater was staring at, but not seeing, the VDU in front of him. Earlier he had sent out a few girls to the big hotels and a string of four to a corporate entertainment bash and then the phone had stopped ringing.

His thoughts were far away; very far away indeed both in time and place, yet they linked with the immediate present.

He was seeing, on the blank screen, a small dusty village on the edge of the Kafue River in Zambia. An old black man with a white clerical collar was ringing a school bell. This was his grandfather, the Reverend Handsome Mutendi. Lysander saw himself and a pack of other small boys, all barefooted, dressed mostly in khaki shirts and shorts, and all carrying slates and slate pencils, follow the old man into the classroom.

This was where Lysander had begun life, on the Kafue Flats. By the time he went to school his father had left to become a soldier and his mother had been killed by an angry buffalo when she went to cut thatching reeds.

Many people had been killed by buffaloes in similar villages along the Kafue. The reason the animals were angry and ready to charge was that, in the local hunting parlance, they were 'carrying lead'.

The village hunters usually possessed little more than muzzle-loading Martini Henris or guns of similar vintage which fired nails, stones, bits of iron and anything else that came to hand.

The buffaloes lived by day in a reed bed a mile wide and three miles long. They came out to drink at night and this was when they were shot at. The charge rarely killed them but it lodged deep and usually turned septic. Carrying lead tended to make them extremely cantankerous.

Goater had always thought of Macrae as a metaphorical buffalo carrying lead, an ill-humoured creature put on earth to harass people like himself. It was well known in Africa that the most dangerous of all game was a buffalo carrying lead.

He had read that Macrae was investigating Julie's torture and murder and knew that he would eventually find the person from the opposite apartment who had seen Frenchy and himself leaving.

There were quite a few black clerics in London but he was sure that if Macrae was given a word association test and the words were 'black churchman', it was an even bet that the first name he would utter would be 'Lysander Goater'.

True, he might then say: Well, he's not a real churchman. But a second later he might say: Let's check him out anyway.

Goater sighed. He did not like calling in the boys, but he had no choice. To win, you had to be cleverer than the buffalo. He lifted the phone and dialled. A woman's voice answered.

'Violet?'

'Yeah.'

'You know who this is?'

'Yeah.'
'OK, let me talk to Jelly.'
'He's sleeping.'
'Let me talk to him, Violet, there's a good girl.'

Chapter Eleven

Macrae stood in his kitchen and sipped his morning coffee. The place was untidy. There were dirty dishes on the table and in the sink. There was nothing in the fridge to eat. The hand of Frenchy was missing.

But he was not thinking about Frenchy's house-wifely duties. He was thinking about her and that bastard Lightly. He had hardly been able to sleep the night before for thinking about it. He hadn't felt jealousy for a long time and didn't even know whether the anger running through his veins *was* jealousy.

He had worked out several scenarios, all of which led back to the fact that Lightly had seen (gone to bed with?) Frenchy at the London Towers, which meant that she had returned to the job she knew best.

Then there was the fact that Lightly was working for Scales on Operation Redlight – the title was one of the Deputy Commander's more lurid aberrations – and was therefore reporting to him.

What had occurred in the pub the night before was simple blackmail: you recommend me for promotion and everything is sweet; you don't – and Scales gets an earful.

Well, he could cope with that. What was making him really angry was the thought of Lightly ordering up a tart for the evening to set in motion an entrapment sting. If he'd gone to bed with Frenchy, he hadn't much of a case; but if he'd set it up and money had changed hands then he had her. And if he had her, he had Macrae; everyone at Cannon Row – except Scales – knew that Frenchy was his woman. And as Les Wilson was continually reminding him, living with a known prostitute meant being axed from the force double quick.

But Macrae had dealt with tougher men than Lightly.

He put his empty coffee cup down, listened to the irregular beat of his heart, shrugged into his coat and went out into the street.

He had been waiting only a matter of minutes before Leo's Golf turned into his road.

'Morning, guv'nor.'

Macrae grunted.

'Where to?'

'The woman's flat.'

Leo drove across Battersea Bridge. The river looked cold and dirty.

Macrae kept silent. In the old days he had had his own driver, Eddie Twyford. But Eddie was dead now and the old days had disappeared under accountants' red pencils. Now detectives of Macrae's rank were supposed to travel by public transport. But Silver, to save his own sanity, had decided he could never accompany Macrae in buses and trains, so he had elected to drive them both in his own car.

He crossed the King's Road. He had come back this way from Laura's flat the previous evening. He thought about the room, the incense, the soft whine of the sitar in the background. He thought of Laura, her bare feet and her long cheese-cloth dress.

He also thought of how he had gone home and settled down for the evening with Zoe and when she had asked him about his day he had not mentioned his visits to the hospital or to Laura.

He told himself it wasn't significant; but that didn't mean he believed it.

He and Macrae spent two hours going through Julia Maddox's flat looking for drugs. They found only an unopened packet of syringes usually supplied to diabetics.

'We know she was on heroin, but there's not a bloody thing,' Macrae said.

'The stuff could still be here, guv'nor.'

'Maybe, but let's say for the moment that she didn't keep it here. That means she was supplied. The supplier came as regular as clockwork. Like the postman. You with me?'

'I think she'd still keep some on the premises.'

'Look, she's got the needles. You can buy these

from any chemist's. But if she was raided they don't prove a thing. Oh! Wait just one wee second.' He picked up the phone, dialled, then asked for Dr Ramsden. When he put the receiver down he said, 'The PM showed no signs of pizza in her stomach.'

'You think—?'

'I think we should find out if anyone else in this block sends out for pizzas. Find out where the nearest pizza places are and ask them. I think we should look in the rubbish bins for empty pizza boxes.'

'And you don't think we'll find any.'

'No, I don't.'

'So we look for the guy who delivers the pizzas that aren't pizzas?'

'Aye, laddie.'

The constable on duty put his head around the door. 'There's a Mr Volker to see you, sir. Says he owns the place.'

A man entered, so vast he made Macrae seem undernourished by comparison. He was in his forties and wore a cheap grey suit. His short hair was grey, so was his skin.

'Mr Volker?' Macrae said.

A voice said, 'Is not Volker, is Boris.'

A small figure, which had been completely obscured by the larger, emerged. He was not more than five feet tall; wore an immaculate double-breasted navy blue overcoat with an astrakhan collar and a black bowler, the kind of hat neither detective had seen for many years. Under the hat was a face so wrinkled and old that for a moment Leo thought that Mr Volker was a chimpanzee.

'Boris is chauffeur,' Volker said.

The fact that he was little more than a midget made no difference to the powerful presence he brought into the room. In Leo's mind a thought stirred.

Volker looked about him at the furniture. He made up his mind. He pointed. Then Leo and Macrae watched fascinated as Boris stepped forward, lifted him as though he was a ventriloquist's dummy, and deposited him in an armchair. His feet, in shiny black boots, did not touch the floor.

'You want to see me, but I come to you,' he said. 'Everything nice. Co-operation.'

'You're not Mr Alois Volker are you, sir?' Leo said.

Volker smiled. The wrinkles grew more pronounced. The eyes closed. 'You know of me?'

'Only what I read in the papers.'

'What is that?'

'Well, that you're . . . that . . . Weren't you on a list of the hundred richest people in Britain? I remember you because you were from one of the Baltic countries. An immigrant. My parents are immigrants. You were number forty-something.'

'Thirty-five. I improve. Boris, I will smoke.'

Boris took out a leather cigar case and Volker selected one. Boris held the match and he drew on it until the cigar was burning to his satisfaction.

'Please excuse,' he said. 'People not like smoking now. They say I must not. My doctor say I must not. But I am too old to stop. You don't mind?'

'No, sir, we don't mind,' Macrae said.

'The lady who was killed. We must speak about it.'

'What we're trying to do is build a profile of her. That's why we spoke to Mr Takorides. But he—'

Volker held up his hand. 'I say to him he must not speak. Boris, the book.'

From a large side-pocket Boris produced a chunky leather-bound book. The small man put on his reading glasses and turned over the pages. 'Takorides, Hector. From Famagusta. Married. Two children. Waiter. Owner small restaurant in Slough. Bankrupt. He working for Volker and Co. five years. No trouble.' He closed the book. 'He is immigrant. I employ immigrant when I can.'

'Are you from Lithuania?' Silver said.

'No, no, my boy. Latvia. I am coming from Riga. But many years ago . . . before you were born . . . before you parents were born. Takorides telephone to me. It is I who say he must not talk to anyone. You must blame me, Mr Policeman. You must put *me* in prison.'

His body shook as he chuckled.

'We don't want to put either of you in prison, sir.'

'Let me say you something. You know how many properties I own? I won't tell. But plenty. These days people do not like landlords. You remember that man who puts dogs into his houses to get people out?'

'In the sixties. Rachman.'

'Yes, Rachman. Since that time people do not like landlords. There are thousands of people living in my buildings. I do not wish publicity. I must be careful of newspapers; of television. You understand?'

'I'm afraid that no matter how careful you are we're still faced with the fact that a woman has been murdered in one of your flats and we want to know about her.'

'That is why I come. I have spoken with Takori-des. He will tell you everything he know. Boris.'

Boris took the cigar and laid it in an ashtray, then, as gently as he had placed him there, he raised Mr Volker from the chair and set him down on his pins.

'I say you good morning,' Volker said.

They watched the two men leave. 'How the hell did you know who he was?' Macrae asked Silver.

'Newspapers, guv'nor.'

'I must have missed it.' He was irritated that Silver knew something he didn't.

'Sir!'

'What is it, Tompkins?'

The young detective, still wearing a nice country-style sports coat and what looked like a school tie, came into the room. His face was shining, his eyes eager.

'Sir, I found this.'

He was holding a small piece of square yellow paper in a dripping hand.

'What is it?'

'A Post-it, sir.'

'A what?'

'One of those notepads with the gum strip,' Silver told him.

'What about it?'

'Well, sir, I needed to go to the loo—' Tompkins said.

'*What?* This is a bloody murder scene! You ask my permission before you take a deep breath, understand?'

'Yes, sir.'

'And it's the lavatory not the loo. Say it!'

'The lavatory, sir.'

'Right. You went to the lavatory. And?'

'I raised the seat because I wanted to—'

'All right . . . all right . . .'

'And this was caught up on the side of the bowl just under the seat. I mean, you had to raise the seat to see it. But when I raised it the paper fell into the water. I think there's been something written on the sheet above it.'

'Let's have a look. No! No! I don't want to touch it. Hold it up. I can't see a thing. Give it to Exhibits Officer. And Tompkins . . . wash your hands.'

'Yes, sir.'

Leo thought his father Manfred would have approved of those sentiments.

When Tompkins had left, Macrae said, 'I'm going to have another go at Takorides. I want you to take a couple of lads and go round the pizza places. Start in the nearby streets and then increase the circle. And they may not have been pizzas. I mean, you see someone coming in with a box you think it's a pizza but it might be some other takeaway: Chinese, Vietnamese, Turkish. OK?'

'Right, guv'nor.'

By mid-afternoon Macrae and Silver were back at Cannon Row in Wilson's office.

Wilson was looking at a folder on his desk advertising holidays in Florida.

'You thinking of going there, Les?'

'Maybe.'

'Buy a gun.'

Wilson swept the bumph into a drawer and said, 'Right. What have we got?'

'Not a lot.' Macrae turned to Silver. 'Go ahead, laddie.'

Silver said, 'There are twelve pizza places, four Chinese takeaways, three doner kebab takeaways, three fish and chip shops, a Vietnamese restaurant that'll do takeaways, no Turkish restaurants, but there is a Greek place. And there are two dinner delivery services but they come with the complete deal: you sit down and they serve.'

'So?'

'No one had orders from Sebastopol Mansions. I don't think they'd even heard of the place.'

Wilson said, 'What about those pizza joints that bring the things on motorbikes. You can order from, oh, I dunno, Acton or Shepherd's Bush, and they're supposed to be there by the time you've put the phone down?'

'Yeah. Harris and Shawcross did those by phone. Nothing.'

'That's great,' Wilson said. 'George? You saw Takorides?'

Macrae nodded. 'She was on the game. He knew it. She was paying him something, probably not a lot, to look the other way. The old man doesn't know that of course and Takorides is scared stiff he'll find out and sack him.'

'Did he admit it?'

'All but.'

'We've seen that film before, George. She needed to feed a habit and there wasn't much else she could do for money.'

'Takorides did confirm the pizza deliveries. He knew what was going on, of course. He was probably getting a cut from the dealer as well.'

'And what's-his-name, Volker, he didn't have a clue?'

'Never,' Macrae said. 'Takorides would have been out on his arse. It'll all come out in the wash, I'm not going to tell him. If he's so bloody rich he can find out himself.'

'You sound like a dangerous socialist, George.'

Macrae ignored him. He picked up a small bin-liner and emptied it on to the table top.

'The usual junk,' he said. 'But one odd thing: we haven't found an address book. Usually get at least one. Her passport is interesting, though. Not the new one,' he prodded a small red passport with his fingertip, 'but the old one.' He picked up the standard dark blue British passport. Its top corner had been cut off by the Passport Office to show that it had expired.

'Look at these stamps, Les: Pakistan, Turkey, Thailand, Cambodia . . .'

'All drug-producing countries.'

'Poppies. Heroin.'

'Anything else?'

'Tompkins found a bit of paper in the lavatory. It was peeled off one of those small yellow notepads and dropped in the bowl. But whoever dropped it in didn't realize it hadn't flushed down. It had got stuck. He says there are indentations on it as though some-one wrote something on the page on top. I couldn't see it myself but he's sent it to Forensic so they might find something.'

'What sort of something?' Wilson said.

'I don't know Les, but if it wasn't S&M – and I don't think it was – then she was tortured. Why?'

'Could have been the dealer. Maybe she was into him for money and he wanted to teach her a lesson and went too far.'

'They don't go in for stuff like that. He'd scar her face; break her arm.'

Silver said, 'Or else someone wanted information. That's the usual way of getting it, isn't it?'

'You've been seeing too many films, laddie,' Macrae said.

'Hang on a second,' Wilson said. 'Go on, Leo.'

'It's only a guess. But if you want information and someone won't give it to you . . .'

'Is that what your parents taught you?' Macrae said. 'What about stuffing her throat full of paper? That's not the best way of getting someone to talk.'

'But one hand was free,' Leo said. 'Maybe she wrote it down.'

Macrae said, 'The yellow paper.'

'Yeah.'

He patted Leo on the shoulder. 'Good lad!'

It was, from Macrae, a kind of Oscar.

'OK,' Wilson said. 'Leo, you keep nagging Forensic.'

The meeting broke up. Macrae stayed behind. 'Les, what do you know of a DS called Lightly?'

'Not a lot.'

'He's been passed over for inspector.'

'Twice. His exams are all right but his personal life . . . well, let's just say it could be better.'

'Sleeping around?'

'No, no, Christ, George, if that was a crime you'd still be a sergeant too. As long as you don't shove it in people's faces, it's all right. No, there've been reports that he gets a bit rough from time to time.'

Macrae paused. He had been known to get rough himself. Then he said, 'With the villains?'

'A couple of tarts. He's been on Vice.'

'Asked me if I would put in a word for him.'

'I wouldn't, George.'

As Leo went through reception the desk sergeant told him there were a couple of messages for him. One was from Zoe. The other was from Laura Parkes saying that her sister was coming to her flat that afternoon and could Leo make it.

He said to the desk sergeant, 'Listen, would you phone Zoe and tell her I may be working late.'

The desk sergeant gave an exaggerated leer. 'If she believes that she'll believe anything.'

Chapter Twelve

Leo reached Putney in the late afternoon and saw Laura on the front steps of her house. As he parked she ran past him down the street. 'Sam!' she shouted, and disappeared around the corner.

He stood beside his car feeling somewhat ridiculous. The street was suddenly empty and he wondered what to do.

Some minutes later she came back. The set of her shoulders and the way she held her head made her look like a waif. She was wearing jeans and a white shirt and as she drew nearer he could see she had been crying.

He spoke to her but she brushed past him and went up the steps to the house. Embarrassed, he followed.

She went into the sitting-room. A tea pot and two cups were on the floor. She picked them up and took them to the kitchen. When she came back she said, 'I'm sorry. You'd better go. Things have changed.'

'You've been crying. Let me help. Is it your sister?'

'I told you. I can't . . . look, you'd better not get mixed up in this . . . I mean I'm grateful but she's . . . sometimes I love her with all my heart and sometimes I think she's a bitch! Mind you, I suppose anyone would be a bitch if they'd gone through what she went through.'

'Well, let me—'

'No.'

'I'm not going to leave you like this. Anything could happen.'

'Like what?'

'Look at your hands.'

She looked at them with interest. They were trembling.

'See what I mean? It could be that you're suffering from some form of post-accident syndrome.'

'Oh, come on.'

'And I feel responsible for what's happening. I mean if I hadn't driven into you . . .'

She smiled. It was a little girl's smile through the tears. 'It's not you or the accident, it's my bloody sister. Didn't you see her as you drove along the street?'

He shook his head.

'She was here until a few minutes ago. I hadn't told her you were a policeman or she wouldn't have come but I thought I'd better when she arrived. The moment I told her she left. I begged her to stay. But she wouldn't.' She smiled again, more like her old self. 'Poor Leo. And you came all this way.'

'It's no big deal. I wanted to . . . see you again and make sure you were OK.'

'I'm fine.'

'Have you had the car looked at?'

'Tomorrow.'

'Promise?'

'I promise.'

'Well . .'

'No, don't go. Have some tea. Let's just talk like civilized human beings. I need to unwind.'

She put on the stereo.

'I love that,' Leo said. 'It's the *Koyaanisqatsi* sound-track, isn't it?' Zoe had bought the tape. He felt a touch of guilt at the association.

Surprised, she said, 'Fancy you knowing it. I love it, too.'

He lay back on the cushions and let the music wash over him. In a few moments she was back with jasmine tea. She sat cross-legged in front of him and they sipped the hot tea in silence.

'To go back to your sister for a moment,' he said. 'Tell her I'll meet her any time. There's no problem. And don't feel guilty about getting me out here. I told you I wanted to see you.'

'You're very sweet . .'

'No, I'm not. But I do know that some people are allergic to coppers even if they haven't done anything wrong.'

'Oh, but she has.'

He raised his eyebrows.

'You see, she's only recently got out of Pucklehurst.'

'The women's prison?'

'Are you shocked?'

'I'm pretty much unshockable. What was she in for?'

'It's a long story.'

'I've got time.'

'I haven't. Not today.'

'When?'

'I'll think about it. I told you it was dirty washing.'

He rose. 'Look, would you like me to see if I can check the computer file anyway for this missing person? Then she needn't ever meet me.'

'Would you? God, I'd be so grateful.'

'Of course. I mean I'll do what I can. What's the person's name?'

'Kendrick. Martin Kendrick. He is . . . was her husband.'

He asked her for details then said, 'OK, leave it with me. I'll ring you if I find anything.'

'Next time I'll offer you something stronger than tea.'

As he drove back along the King's Road he heard that last sentence over and over in his mind. Was there a subtext to it? What was she implying?

'It's moving,' Mrs Pinker whispered. 'Can you feel it?'

'Only a little,' Frenchy said.

'Give it time.'

Frenchy and her mother were sitting at the round dining table in Mrs Pinker's semi in South London. The planchette on its little wheels was on a sheet of white paper. The women had their fingers on the board. The curtains were closed, the room was in semi-darkness. In the half light Mrs Pinker, in a silver jump suit topped by a white wig, shone like a beacon.

'There it goes again,' she whispered.

This time Frenchy sensed it and heard the scrape of the pencil point on the paper. She felt a sense of excitement and wonder. She had never really believed in automatic writing but here it was; no doubt about it.

The planchette wrote for some seconds and then stopped.

'Is that all?' Frenchy said.

'I dunno. Let's see what it says.'

She switched on the light and they looked at the paper. There were a number of squiggles then one that looked like a word.

'Glask,' Frenchy said.

Mrs Pinker examined it carefully. 'Could be George.'

'Never. That doesn't look like a George. Anyway you was never married to a George. Frank, Bill and Chris. That's what you told me.'

Mrs Pinker's eyes went into long focus. 'Frank . . . he was a lovely man. Always brought a packet of prawns home of a Friday night. Prawns and brown ale . . . And then . . . well, I won't tell you what happened then.'

'I thought he was having it off with someone else.'

'I didn't know that, did I? Anyway it would've finished when he got five years for robbery with violence. After him came your father. He was good to me too. Then they got him for that bank job in Acton and that was the end of him. He says to me, 'Get on with your own life, Norah. Don't wait for me.' So I did. Then came Chris. I never liked him much. No style. Petty thieving, that was about his mark.'

'You don't even know if they're dead or alive.'

'But *they* know.'

'What's that supposed to mean?'

'Stands to reason if they're dead they got to be on the other side, and you know everything when you're on the other side.'

'Everything? There's millions of people on the other side. Millions and millions. Think how many have died since the world started.'

'Not died. We don't say died.'

'Passed over then. I mean how's Frank going to know you're trying to get in touch with him?'

'He'll just know,' Mrs Pinker said, mysteriously.

'And for God's sake, Mum, why? What you want to get in touch *for*?'

'Because I'm lonely, that's why. I need a man. Always have done.'

Mrs Pinker lit a cigarette and left it between her lips. In the light it was possible to see that the wig had become discoloured on one side from the constant rising smoke. She squinted through it at the paper.

'Glask,' she said. 'No . . . doesn't sound like anything.'

'Sounds like a car part to me.'

'That's gask. Something like that. Turn it round . . .'

'Ksalg . . .' Frenchy said. 'I suppose you could say that's getting closer to Chris.'

Mrs Pinker turned the paper this way and that. 'What would you say if I was to get married again?'

'I'd say you was going soft in the head.'

'You don't understand. You've got your copper to keep you warm at night. Someone there when you wake up at three o'clock in the morning.'

'You got someone in mind?'

'Not really. I'm hoping planchette will write a name.'

'Well, his name is Glask. Mr Glask. All you got to do now is find him.'

'Couldn't be flask, could it?'

'Mr Flask then. You could ask at bingo. Is there a Mr Flask in the house?'

'Highly amusing. Let's have another go.'

Frenchy looked at her watch. 'Can't stop.'

'Class?'

'Yeah.'

'I don't want no broken arms, so you take care.'

Frenchy kissed her mother's head and went upstairs to change. When she came down Mrs Pinker was sitting hunched over the table, her hands on the board, the room in semi-darkness again.

The car was a black 1977 Trans Am with a shark's head on the engine cover. The shark had its mouth open as though ready to devour the nearest pedestrian. But there were few pedestrians in Queensway on this cold autumn night.

Inside the Trans Am, Jellicoe Brothers and Big Boy Truscott smoked and chewed gum. Jelly wore a leather flying jacket with *Shaman Dancer* stencilled on the back, Big Boy wore an army combat jacket with a pocket which bulged dangerously.

Big Boy was tall and thin and mournful looking, a kind of Damon Runyon figure lost in London. Jelly was short and squat and had a range of deltoids on which he could have balanced plates. Years before, when he had been no more than a child, he had seen pictures of the diminutive British weight-lifter Precious Mackenzie and had found his role model.

They had been sitting in Queensway for nearly an hour and both were cold. They had shared a joint, they had discussed what they were going to do to Violet if she didn't get her act together and clean up the house, they had stared out of the windows at the nearby restaurants and smelled the inviting smell of Peking duck.

'He keep me waitin' he goin' be sorry,' Big Boy said.

'He goin' be sorry anyhow,' Jelly said. 'Very sorry.'

'You hear what Lysander said. No killing. No mutilation.'

'I ain't goin' waste 'im.'

'I don't like that friggin' Lysander.'

'You don't have to like him. We enforce . . .' He dwelt lovingly on the word – for that's how Jelly saw himself: an enforcer. 'We enforce, he pays, end of story. That him comin' now?' He pointed to a small Hiace van.

'See what it say.'

The van drew level with the Trans Am and they saw the registration.

'Yeah, that's him.'

Big Boy let the van get half a block and two cars ahead, then pulled out into the stream. The Trans Am's big 6.6 litre V8 engine throbbed menacingly. Big Boy kept the revs down and tooled it along Queensway.

The van bustled on a couple of blocks then stopped in Craven Street. A young man jumped out, opened the back, took out a flat box, relocked the back and went into a house. In a few moments he was back.

Big Boy and Jelly watched and waited. The van drove up to the Bayswater Road and headed in the direction of Notting Hill. It stopped at a block of flats. Here the lights were bright and the two enforcers got a good view of the driver. He was young and dressed in a shiny jacket with *Boston Wolves* stencilled on the back, a baseball cap turned backwards and Reeboks. He went through the same process.

Next stop Lancaster Gate. The van drew up outside a house off Inverness Terrace. Big Boy nosed the Trans Am up to its rear and, as the driver got out, so did Jelly.

Jelly said, 'You sellin' pizzas?'

The young driver shook his head. 'I ain't sellin' nothin'.'

'We seen you deliver. We hungry,' Big Boy said.

'These are orders.'

'I givin' orders.' Jelly grabbed him. As he did so a pistol appeared in the youth's hand. But Jelly was waiting. He grasped the hand and squeezed until bones began to crack. Big Boy took the pistol.

'What your name?' Jelly said.

'Fuck you.'

'That a nice name.'

He squeezed again.

'Oh, Jesus. Rolo.'

'OK, Rolo. Open up.'

'They goin' to do you, man.'

'They?'

'Yeah, they.'

'Open up.'

Rolo's hand was crushed again and this time the pain made him almost faint. Big Boy took his keys and opened the rear of the van where there was a neat pile of pizza boxes. On the lids was the slogan

Wells Fargo Pizzas. We always get thru. Big Boy ripped open one labelled *American Hot. With jalapeños.* It looked good enough to eat even though it was cold. He tore it apart.

'Yeah . . . Yeah . . . Yeah . .' he said.

'He gonna kill you, man,' Rolo said.

'Oh, he, not they.'

Big Boy said, 'Wells Fargo always get through, hey? Well, the Mounties always get their man.'

They pushed Rolo's head against the railings of a house. Jelly pulled them apart slightly.

'Oh, Jesus!' Rolo said.

'Listen, you tell us who he is an' you're OK. You don't an' you goin' through.'

'Honest to God, I—'

'You goin' through, then.'

'Please . . . please . . . all I know is his first name. Mike.'

'Where does he live?'

'I dunno.'

'Where you pick up the stuff?'

'Different places. I get a call.'

'You goin' through.'

'No! No! If I knew I'd tell you.'

'Tough shit.'

They pushed his head through the railings. Even Jelly's strength was not able to bend the iron bars more than a little and Rolo lost part of an ear. He wasn't aware of the loss at that time because by then he was unconscious.

'Have a nice night,' Jelly said.

'You want to take the van?' Big Boy said.

'You like pizzas?'

'I love pizzas. Specially American hot.' He smiled for the first time that evening.

Chapter Thirteen

The day was raw with a wind from the north-east and squalls of thin, driving rain. Macrae, in the passenger seat of Silver's car, stared out at the countryside. It was a landscape of newly ploughed fields and woods, of great beech trees which had lost most of their leaves.

'Hampshire.' Leo pointed to a county boundary sign at the side of the road.

Macrae grunted. After a few moments he said, 'Eddie hated the countryside.'

Leo smiled at the memory of Macrae's late driver. 'Eddie hated anything that wasn't in the West End or the City. He loved diesel fumes and petrol fumes. I think he was scared of the countryside. All that fresh air. Don't you miss it, guv'nor?'

'Why the hell should I miss it?'

'Well . . . I mean, coming from Scotland. That's pretty much all countryside, isn't it?'

'Have you ever been to the Highlands?'

'Edinburgh's as far north as I've been.'

'You should go sometime. That's real countryside. Mountains and rivers and lochs. Not like this place, gentrified, prettified, dandyfied. It's for wee girls with ponies. The Volvo bloody set – there's the sign.'

The sign read: 'Royal Hampshire Golf Course. Please drive carefully.'

They wound their way along a small road. They were in different country now. There was heather and pine trees and substantial houses discreetly hidden behind high hedges. After a few minutes they came to the golf course itself.

On a lovely summer's day it would have been a picture, but on a cold windy morning in late autumn it looked uninviting. The club house was a long low thatched building that overlooked the first tee and the eighteenth green. Now, at mid-morning, the only golfer in sight was a man in an all-weather suit practising chipping.

The car park was almost empty and the two detectives hurried towards the club house. The figure on the practice green straightened up and came towards them. He was a gaunt man in his sixties with a neatly trimmed white moustache.

'Looking for a game?' he said.

'No . . . no . . .' Macrae began, 'we—'

'Can't say I blame you. Rotten bloody weather. Been like this for weeks. You'll soon need webbed toes to play here. Worst year I can remember and last year they were talking about drought. It's all this praying for rain. Look what's happened now.' He pointed to the dark clouds moving swiftly overhead. 'And so bloody cold you can't grip the clubs properly. Are you looking for someone?'

'Colonel Maddox.'

'Oh?'

'He's the secretary, isn't he?'

'Yes I am. What can I do for you?'

Macrae held out his warrant card.

'Oh, Christ,' the colonel said. 'You've come about Julia.'

'That's right, sir.'

'Were you the one who rang and told me?'

'No, sir, that'd be my chief superintendent.'

'Come in then.'

They followed him into a large office in the deserted club house. He stripped off his weather-proofs and threw them into a corner.

'You'd better sit down,' he said. 'What is it you want to know?'

'Anything and everything, sir. We're trying to build up a picture of her.'

The colonel pulled open a drawer and took out a bottle of Scotch and three glasses. 'You'll take a nip?'

'Not for me, thanks,' Leo said.

Macrae shook his head. 'It's a wee bit early for me.'

Leo looked at him in surprise.

'A wee bit early is it, Inspector?' The colonel's face twisted in sudden anger. 'A wee bit early?' He poured half a glass and took a hefty swig. 'It's not too early for me. There's nothing like a drop of whisky to take away the pain, don't you think?'

'I'm sure you're right, sir.'

'Yes, I am bloody right. Anything and everything. Well, that's a tall order. Why come to me? I'm only the father. What the hell am I supposed to know!' He drank again. 'You want to build up a picture of her? When you do maybe you'll show it to me. No . . . better not . . . I don't want to know. All right, fire away.'

'When did you last see her?'

'In the morgue, where do you think? I had to identify her. Have you ever had to identify a dead body, Inspector? I have. Several times. Two in the army. A corporal and a ranker who were squashed by a tank. That was in sixty . . . sixty-something. Can't remember. And then there was Olive. That was my wife. Multiple pile-up on the motorway . . .'

The two detectives were seated, but the colonel was pacing up and down. As he went over to the big picture window he stumbled and Leo guessed he had been drinking earlier.

'Olive gone. Julia gone. I buried my father last year. Last of the Mohicans, that's me . . .'

'Before she died, sir. That's what I meant.'

'I had lunch with her after she came back from the Far East. That was years ago, when she was going round with that shit what's-his-name. She didn't choose to see me after that so I didn't choose to see her.'

'How many years ago was that?' Macrae said.

'Oh, ten, a dozen.'

'She was in London and you were—'

'Here.'

'And her mother?'

'Her mother was dead by then. In a way I'm glad. This would have done for her. She loved Julia. Spoiled her. I used to say, look, we've told her no. We must stick to it . . .'

'To what, sir?'

'What?'

'You told her no to what?'

'Any bloody thing, whatever I didn't want her to do: stay out late, smoke, drink, go around with unsuitable boys: all that sort of thing. Olive used to say but if we don't let her she'll do it all the same and lie. I said you have to have an objective for your children. That's what life's all about. You analyse what you want them to achieve. Then you set out the parameters within which they'll achieve that goal. Olive didn't. I did. Have you any children, Inspector?'

'Yes, sir, three. And it's superintendent.'

Rank was something the colonel valued. 'I do apologize. To go back to what we were saying – if you have a daughter you'll know exactly what I'm talking about.'

Macrae thought briefly of his grown-up daughter Susan, herself out in the Far East, and the two younger children, Margaret and Bobby. Had he been like this man he wondered? Had he also set out parameters for life's targets like some behavioural gunlayer on a firing range? He didn't think so but only their mothers could really answer that.

'I mean, you take schooling,' Colonel Maddox said. 'I was in Germany with NATO. So naturally she came back to boarding school in England. She hated it. Tried to run away a couple of times. Things went from bad to worse. Shoplifting. Smoking marijuana – at fourteen mind you – until finally she was expelled.

'My wife went back to England to be with her. Left me high and dry in Germany, took a house in Surrey and sent her to a local school as a day pupil. You know how long we were separated? Two bloody years. I only saw her on leaves. Two years. And we were in the prime of our lives!'

He stared out at a two-ball struggling up the eighteenth in the wind.

'D'you know what two years apart can do to a marriage?'

'I can guess,' Macrae said.

'And you'd be right.

'After Julia left school and when I came back to England she lay about the house. I used to say, "For God's sake, is this how you're going to spend the rest of your life?" And do you know what she said? She said she didn't know! Hadn't made up her mind! In the army you make decisions. They may be the wrong decisions but at least you act. Any decision is better than no decision.'

Again he paused, then he said, 'The point is, I did my best. And look what happened. I mean why . . .? Why . . .?'

Suddenly he broke. He turned away. His shoulders shook and the sobs, bitten back, came out as hisses.

The two detectives were silent.

He took out a red and white spotted handkerchief and blew his nose. 'Sorry about that but the booze also makes one vulnerable to this sort of thing.' He pulled himself upright, straightening his shoulders and tucking his chin in as though on parade. 'I'm all right now.'

'What we really want to know is about her friends and her lifestyle,' Macrae said. 'The more we can find out the more hope we have. It was a terrible crime, sir.'

'Yes, it was. Bloody frightful. If I ever caught the shit who did it I'd castrate him. No anaesthetic. Just tie him up as he tied her up and cut his balls off. And then I'd shoot him in the knees. And then—'

'You mentioned someone, a man, you said she'd come back from the Far East with him. Can you remember his name, or anything else about him?'

'I only met him the once. About Julia's age. Michael somebody. Don't think I ever knew his surname. Hated him on sight. Long hair tied back. Long nails. Baggy suit. Supposed to be very chic I imagine, but it looked ridiculous.'

'Were they . . .?' Leo began.

'What?'

'Partners?'

'Partners! Do you mean were they sleeping together? How the hell should I know? You don't ask your daughter questions like that. But I should think so. And probably sticking needles into one another as well.'

'Was she an addict, then?' Macrae said.

'God knows. She was as thin as a rail, though. We had lunch together in Soho. She hardly ate a thing. Pushed her food around on her plate. Jerky and nervous. Kept on looking over my shoulder at the street outside as though she was waiting for someone. I said, "Listen, if you've got something better to do then go and do it, don't let me keep you." And she smiled a sad smile and got up and kissed me on the cheek and said, "Sorry, Daddy." That's the last thing she ever said to me: "Sorry, Daddy." Christ . . .'

They talked for a further forty minutes and then Macrae and Leo left for London.

'Well, so much for the bloody colonel,' Macrae said.

Leo said, 'Takorides, the foot doctor, the colonel . . . we're not getting very far, guv'nor.'

Macrae did not even bother to grunt.

DCS Wilson pulled the perforated strips from the computer sheet and dropped them in his waste-basket. Then he studied the page. Macrae and Silver watched him.

'Julia Eleanor Maddox,' he read. Then to Macrae, 'You were right, George, she was about thirty. Thirty-one in fact . . ' He flicked the paper with his finger. 'The US Drug Enforcement Agency has a file on her, so has Interpol. Let's see: Pakistan, Turkey, Thailand, Australia. They match her passport all right.' He flicked the paper again. 'Charged in Perth. Acquitted. Arrested in Johannesburg. Released then deported. Arrested in Spain. No charge. And so it goes on. Interpol says she was treated for addiction in France. Four months in a clinic in Paris. A month later picked up by the police in Marseilles. Overdose. Treated in hospital . . . No convictions . . . A lucky girl, our Julia . . .'

'I wouldn't call what happened to her lucky,' Macrae said.

'No, that's true. What have you got, George?' Wilson said.

'We saw her father. A colonel. Golf club secretary. You know the type. He's pretty broken up. But you can see why she took the road she did. I would've too, with him as a father. The trouble is he didn't see his daughter for years, so he's out of touch. He did mention someone called Michael but no surname.'

'What was he?'

'Boyfriend. He came back with her from the Far East.'

'So nothing much there.'

'Not much. But Rogerson went through the dustbins at her flat and found a pizza. Made by something called the Wells Fargo Pizza Company, according to the box. Not listed. Anyway, the pizza was broken in half but nothing was eaten so that must be how the drugs got to her. We've got a call out for anyone who knows anything about this Wells Fargo operation.'

'She was a tart, wasn't she?' Wilson said.

'That's what it looks like.'

'What about that pimp of yours? Goaty?'

'You owe me a pint for that,' Macrae said. 'First time I've ever heard you get a name wrong.'

'Not Goaty?'

'Goater.'

'He's been an informant before, hasn't he?'

'Once or twice. Reluctantly. I'll try him though.'

'While you were playing golf with the colonel the pathologist phoned. He says she was struck a blow on the neck. Probably knocked her out or incapacitated her for some minutes.'

'Just long enough for him to tie her up.'

'Probably.'

'Anything on that piece of paper Tompkins found in the lavatory?'

'Nothing yet. I'll get on to Forensic.'

The meeting broke up. As Leo walked past the desk sergeant he said, 'Any messages?'

'Not a thing. Your girlfriend must have got sick of you.'

'Phone Zoe for me, would you? I might be late.'

'Where shall I say you are?'
'Solving crime.'
'Very funny.'

Chapter Fourteen

Leo rang and knocked at Laura's door. He was turning away when he saw her jogging along the street towards him. She was wearing the same dark blue track suit she'd had on the day of the accident and her hair was tied back in a pony tail. Her face was flushed from the run and she looked about sixteen.

As she saw him her face broke into a smile. It had all the warmth he recalled from the hospital.

'I was passing,' he said.

'I'm glad. I almost phoned you. Come in.'

He smelled the hot sweat from her body. It wasn't like men's sweat but was mixed with other, more subtle smells. She switched on the lights in the sitting-room. 'You go in. I must change, then we'll have a drink.'

He wandered round the room. He heard the shower, an intimate sound, as though he was not a stranger any longer.

He looked at the ornaments on the walls; the nose flute, the finger drums, the lute-like instrument. The room smelled of stale incense and, on closer examination, he saw that the walls were grimy. Typical London, he thought, never look too closely.

She was back in fifteen minutes. She had put on a long towelling gown and was still drying her hair.

'I've been a good girl,' she said. 'I've done my exercise for the day. Now I can be a bad girl and have a drink.'

'The yin and yang of modern life,' Leo said.

She looked up at him sharply. 'You practise that?'

'No. I've read about it.'

'Oh. Tequila?'

She came back with a bottle, salt and lemon slices.

'I forget which to take first,' he said.

'Salt first.' She poured a little in the hollow behind his right thumb, then gave him a small glass of neat tequila. She held her glass up and stared at him over the rim, then she drank, and sucked the lemon. He copied her. The salt made his mouth slightly numb and the liquor seemed to have little taste.

'Do you like it?'

'Yes. To tell you the truth I've hardly ever had it,' he said.

She took a pouch off a low table and began to roll a joint. 'Should I be doing this? I mean, you're a policeman.'

'I've smoked,' he said.

She lit, inhaled and passed it to him. He sucked in the smoke and as the drug took effect he felt a gentle lassitude. They had another drink and passed the joint back and forth. After a while he lay back on the cushions and smiled at the ceiling.

He had been putting off talking about her sister but now, his inhibitions released, he said, 'I checked the missing persons register. There's nobody on it by the name of Kendrick.'

'Oh.' The way she said it made him feel he had failed her. 'She'll be disappointed.'

'There was only a slim chance.'

'I know, but she clings to things like that. It's all she has in life.'

'Didn't he visit her in Pucklehurst?'

'Sam hasn't seen him for years. He never visited her in prison. Not once.'

'He sounds like a bastard.'

'He is.'

'Why does she want to find him, then?'

'She's destitute, Leo. I do what I can. But I'm on a knife edge myself. She gets a handout from the state but she hates it.'

'I can understand that.'

'Is there no other way?'

'Not really. What was she in for?'

'Smuggling drugs. But she's innocent.' She saw the expression on his face and said, 'Everyone says that, right?'

'Almost everyone.'

'I'm her sister and I *know*. She was set up.' She paused. 'Oh, dear, they all say that too, don't they?'

'Look, I'll—'

'But she didn't do it, Leo! She swore to me and I believe her.'

There was a passion in her voice he hadn't heard before.

'Is there no other way of finding him?' she said. 'Aren't there any other lists of people? We keep on hearing about the marvellous computer the police use.'

'The Holmes Computer?'

'Whatever it's called.'

He shook his head. 'There've been too many breaches of security lately. Too many people have been asking favours. That information is kept pretty tight.'

'Even from people like you?'

'I'd have to have a reason. I assume you're thinking of tracing him through previous convictions. Something like that?'

'I don't know what I'm thinking of. I just know that the police have information about a great many people. But if it's a problem, forget it.'

He didn't reply. She got up and put on a tape. The sound of drumming, very soft at first, filled the room. Gradually it grew louder. It was an intricate rhythm on a finger drum and it combined with the drug to produce in him a strange excitement.

'Do you like it?' she said.

'What is it?'

'Tablas. This is a raga.'

What happened next seemed in retrospect part of an inevitable chain, which had begun to form with the accident, the visit to the hospital, his first visit to her flat.

She moved back from the stereo and her fingers touched his head. She said, 'Thank you, anyway.'

He caught her hand and brought it to his lips.

'That's very sweet,' she said. 'The gentil parfit knight.'

Her robe had come undone and he saw that she was naked. She was smelling of scented soap and powder and he pulled her towards him and kissed her. Even as he did so it was as though he was standing outside his own body watching what was happening there on the big cushions, and part of his mind was saying, don't do this, and another part was saying, yes . . . you must . . .

She started to undress him: first his shirt and then his trousers. He felt her hand in his groin.

'Quickly,' she said.

Her mouth was on his stomach.

'Don't bite me,' he said.

She seemed to freeze. 'I don't bite.'

He penetrated her, but something had gone wrong. He tried, they both tried, but after a while he stopped and neither was satisfied.

They lay back against the cushions. 'I'm sorry,' he said.

She rose on her elbow and kissed him gently. 'Leo, it would be a miracle if it worked the first time.

It almost never does. But I enjoyed it. I wanted to hold you and I wanted you to hold me. Next time it'll be better. And the time after that better still.'

She pulled the robe around her and went out of the room. When she came back she was dressed in jeans and a sweat shirt and she was carrying two more drinks.

For Leo the magic had gone. He looked at his watch and saw her frown as she noticed. This was a cliché of married men, he thought: the evening with the mistress, the drinks, the sex, then the covert glance at the time.

As though to help him she said, 'Leo, I'm really sorry but I've got to go out.'

'No problem. I should be getting along myself.'

'And don't worry about the other thing.'

'I'll make some enquiries. See how the land lies.'

'You were asking about Sam and I never really was able to explain.' She went to a cupboard and took out a thick A4 refill pad. The cover was scuffed and had small tears in it. 'Read it. She kept a diary and then in Pucklehurst rewrote it and turned the whole thing into a journal.'

He took the pad, glad to be offered an easy way out.

'I'll call you,' he said.

In the car going back to Pimlico he felt succeeding waves of emotion: guilt, a kind of elation at what had just occurred, then disappointment at his clumsy performance.

It wasn't late when he got home but Zoe was asleep. He showered and inspected his shirt. There were no lipstick marks on it and he hadn't expected to find any for she did not wear lipstick. He sniffed it. It smelled of a mixture of his own sweat and her perfumed soap and incense. He put it in the bottom of a plastic bag, emptied the kitchen rubbish on to it and took it down to the bins in the basement of the house. If he went on like this it was going to be an expensive affair.

But he wasn't going on with it, was he?

He went back upstairs and Zoe called him into the bedroom. She was sleepy and the room was in semi-darkness.

'Get your clothes off,' she said. 'I've been waiting for you.'

'It's no good tonight.'

'Don't tell me you've got a "headache".'

'I'm exhausted, that's all. It's this bloody case.'

She rose on one elbow. 'Are you all right, Leo?'

'I'm fine.'

'You don't sound fine.'

'For Christ's sake!'

'You haven't been the Leopold Silver I used to know for the past few days.'

'I'm sorry. I think it started with the accident.'

'For God's sake, get yourself together. Nothing happened. Nothing is going to happen. Period. Now if you're not coming to bed, I'm going back to sleep.'

She turned over and Leo went downstairs.

The guilt was gripping him more tightly. He poured himself a glass of red wine. He slumped down in his chair and turned to the first page of Samantha's journal.

The Naked Diary. That's what I called this. But it's a Journal now. There are parts that are naked and parts that have been softened and dressed up, but at least it's the truth.

And even if no one believes me I'll know it is.

So where to start? Birth? No. Let's start at the other end: the beginning of death. That would be Heathrow and the plane to Bangkok.

As I queued at boarding I thought: he should be here. This was his idea to start with, not mine. Let's go to Thailand, he'd said. Let's, I said, and I'd sold my skis and stereo to pay for the ticket. All he'd done was ask his mother for the money.

Enough of him. Let's go.

First stop Amsterdam. It's mid-afternoon when we leave there, but the Thai stewardesses pretend it's night-time. All the blinds get drawn. We have dinner. We watch the movie.

It didn't work for me. I didn't sleep. I realized something: I was doing it to spite him; I didn't really want to be there.

Nor in Bangkok either. You think it's all those lovely old buildings like Chinese pagodas but it's more like parts of LA or Torremolinos. Junk buildings.

Junk men.

And they're all pushing their goddam faces into mine and shouting taxis and hotels and Christ knows what.

And heat.

Was there ever heat like this? Wet heat. And filthy air. If you bottled the air it would condense into a brown fluid.

So I said screw you and found a desk where I ordered a taxi and went off in an old Mazda which was air conditioned, thank God.

NOTE: That's pretty much Naked Diary. How I felt then. And it wasn't Thailand that was the problem, it was me. But this is MY magic carpet, OK?

So let me tell you about the mysterious East. It took three hours to get into Bangkok, the traffic was so heavy. You want to know what I saw? Freeways, construction sites, and billboards advertising McDonald's, Pizza Hut and Baskin Robbins ice cream. I saw one golden Buddha; it was tied on the back of a pick-up truck.

OK, it was a time warp after our day-for-night flight and I was feeling disoriented but it didn't help when the taxi driver ripped me off. We no agree price . . . we no agree price . . . He kept on saying that as he upped the fare.

The Khao San Road . . . we'd talked about it, the Bastard and me. We'd read about it. We'd made pictures in our minds. This was it, man, this was where everyone went.

It was smaller and dirtier than I had imagined. And I hadn't been out of the taxi for more than a minute when the sky opened.

That's how it happens there. The big purple clouds open. The word rain doesn't describe it. It's falling water. Heavy. Drenching. In two seconds I was wet like I'd dived into a pool. But hot too. Air-con, the hotels said. But I didn't have money for hotels.

It was so dark it was like night. The falling water was so heavy I could see nothing. I tried to lift my pack but it was waterlogged and weighed a ton.

That was almost the last time I thought of him. God damn you! I cried. Why aren't you here?

And a voice said, 'You English?'

It came from a shop doorway.

'Let me help you.'

And she ran out and helped me to shelter.

In half an hour she had booked me into the Milky Way Guest House, 90 baht (less than £3 a night with fan, shower and squat loo), and we were having a coffee in the Paradise Bar while the water continued to fall.

Jane. That was her name.

If I had been a praying sort of person I would have thanked the golden Buddha for her.

She was from London. A few years older than me. Tall and slender and attractive. She'd come over with her boyfriend but he'd wanted to go on to Bali and she'd said no and he'd said yes and that had been that.

We were alike.

I told her about HIM and she said he sounded like a bastard.

Magic.

We stayed in the Paradise Bar while the water fell

and we had something to eat. She knew about the food, like those prawns done in chilli sauce that I'd only read about. When it came to paying we split the bill in half like old friends do.

I slept well. The mattress was still covered in plastic. My room was clean. It was on the third floor – the second really because in Thailand the ground floor is called first – and Jane slept above me. There were stairs everywhere and they all led to a series of hallways which surrounded a courtyard. Everywhere you looked were balconies screened by washing. Everywhere were kittens and the kittens lived on cockroaches.

On my first day in Bangkok I had four showers but soon I got used to the heat. Jane said you got used to it or you dropped. We spent the day together. She knew the place well and we travelled by tuk-tuk, the three-wheelers which are open at the sides. God knows where we went but we ended up at Wat Po for a massage and while old men climbed about our bodies and pushed our joints in strange directions, Jane said we should eat together. I had the chilli prawns again. Then she gave me a small bunch of flowers and said they were a goodbye present. She was leaving next day.

NOTE: You don't know how things affect you till they happen. It was like a death in the family.

Leaving? Leaving? Back to London?

No, she was going to one of the islands for a few days, then home.

By herself?

Sure. Her own Bastard was supposed to have gone

154

*with her but he'd be in Bali now so she was going
by herself.*

Did she want to go by herself?

Not really.

*Would she like a little company? Someone who
wouldn't be pushy; who would be there but not be there
if she knew what I meant.*

*She smiled as though she was my greatest friend in
the entire world and said she had hoped I might come
with her but she hadn't liked to ask.*

*We travelled in an old air-con Mercedes bus through
the falling water. The air-con was just airvents like you
have on planes but at least it was something because
the heat was worse than I'd ever known. I stuck to the
seat and then, as I began to sweat, I slithered about on
the plastic surface.*

*I slept as though I had fever and there were dreams
to match.*

*At six o'clock in the morning we arrived on the
West Coast and took the ferry to Koh Phan-Hgan and
Ban Khai.*

You want paradise? Ban Khai is paradise.

*You know those old black and white movies where
Hollywood builds the lotus island on the back lot? This
was Hollywood. A small island, few roads, waterfalls,
jungle, temples, palm trees, white sands – and all surrounded by the clearest and cleanest of blue seas.*

*We went to the Waterfall Bungalows. They were
Hollywood too. One 'bungalow' per person. Each was a
hut made of leaves with a shower and a hammock.*

What more did you want from life? Jane said.

By the time we got there my life was already changed beyond reclamation.

Only I didn't know it.

Chapter Fifteen

'George?'

He knew the voice on the phone instantly; it was his first wife.

'Hello, Linda.'

'Sorry if I got you up.'

'No, no, I was up.'

Up, in the continued absence of Frenchy, meant picking his way around a filthy kitchen trying to find a clean receptacle for coffee.

'I wanted to catch you before you went to work.'

'Is something wrong?' As he said it he felt his heart lurch, then plunge into silence. *Come on!*

'No, not at all, but I've heard from Susan and I wanted to let you know.'

Their daughter had been on an extended trip to the Far East and Australia for more than a year.

'Is she all right?'

'She's fine. She's coming home.'

'That's good.'

He waited for Linda to say something about the need for money – why else would she phone? –

and his heart continued to thump irregularly. The expenses of his daughter's trip and the money he had borrowed to pay for it had nearly cost him his life.*

'And you don't have to worry about money.'

He thought he had misheard. 'What was that?'

'Truly. Apparently she's been working in a pub in Sydney and has saved enough. Did you hear me?'

'Aye. I heard. What about what's-his-name? The boy she was with?'

'She's still with him. That's good, isn't it?'

'I suppose so. When does she arrive?'

'Not tomorrow or even next week. Says she's coming home by way of Africa. She'll spend a couple of weeks there.' He did not reply and she said, 'George?'

'Aye.'

'I thought you'd gone.'

The sound and quality of her voice had started all the old trains running. He tried to visualize her. Would she be in a night-dress? He remembered what she looked like in a night-dress, remembered it vividly, for she was the first woman he had ever seen in one. He remembered her body, thin and wiry at first then softer and fuller as she grew into motherhood.

That was all more than twenty years ago and he

Never Die in January by Alan Scholefield (Pan Macmillan).

thought for the thousandth time what a fool he'd been to let her go.

Except that wasn't accurate.

Not *let her go*. To think like that was just the old bullshit. She'd had no alternative but to leave after he'd started getting his leg over Mandy. Now Mandy was the second ex-Mrs Macrae and had two kids to prove it. But unlike his feelings for Linda, he had never seriously wanted her back.

'Listen,' he said. 'Would you have dinner with me some night this week? Any night.'

'I . . . I'm . .' she paused. 'George, I could say I don't have a free evening but that's not true. I just don't think it's a good idea. Let's wait till Susan gets back and then maybe think about the three of us. What do you say?'

'Well . . . Oh aye, all right, if that's what you want.'

'I think that'll be better. Goodbye George.'

He put down the phone and took his coffee into the sitting-room. The curtains were still drawn and he flung them back and stared out at the grey street. He wondered if she was still having it off with that bloody writer who'd moved into an adjoining flat.

Then he wondered about Susan.

Then he wondered about Frenchy.

And that shaped his actions.

He got dressed, went out to his car and opened the glove compartment. He took out a London street directory and looked up an address in Acton, then he drove north.

Clematis Court had probably been built on a bomb site in the 1950s: red brick, balconies with hanging washing, six flats in all. Not exactly the kind of place Macrae would have chosen to live. He parked, went into the building and rang the bell of number three. A dirty net curtain on what might have been the kitchen window flicked but that was all. He rang again. This time the door opened fractionally, held on a chain. It was unlike any door chain he had seen. This wasn't your brass ornament, this was case-hardened steel that would have laughed at the average bolt cutters.

'Yes?'

He dropped his eyes to child level. She was eight or nine, thin, pale, with frightened eyes.

'Hello,' he said.

'Yes?' she repeated.

He saw the net curtain jerk again and heard a woman's voice but could not make out what she said.

The door began to close.

'Please,' he said.

'What?'

'Don't close it. Is your mother in?'

There was a slight pause and the child said, 'No.'

'You shouldn't say that,' Macrae said. 'Even if it's true, never tell a stranger you're alone.'

The child looked at him as though he had come from an asteroid.

'What's your name?' Macrae said. The door began to close again and he put his hand on the frame.

'You'll break my fingers if you close it.'

The girl stared at him. A voice behind her said, 'If you don't go away I'll call the police.'

'Mrs Lightly?'

'Who are you? Why are you here?'

'I'm George Macrae. I work with your husband.'

'I don't want anyone inside.'

'I'm not anyone.' He held up his warrant card so she could see it.

'What do you want?'

'To tell you the truth, Mrs Lightly, I'd like to meet you. Your husband's got a promotion board in a couple of weeks and he's asked me to help him. He wants promotion from sergeant to inspector.'

'I know all about that.'

'You wouldn't want him to think you weren't going to co-operate, would you?'

She didn't reply.

'Wives are important to their husbands' careers these days. Much more than before.'

'I don't want to talk to you. I don't feel up to it.'

'Are you ill? Would you like me to call a doctor?'

'No.'

'I could put a call through to your husband on the car radio. I'm sure he'd want to come home if you had a problem.'

Abruptly the child was drawn back and the door was closed. He waited to hear the chain being slipped preparatory to the door opening fully, but nothing happened.

'Mrs Lightly?'

She did not reply.

He called, 'If you're not feeling well we'll leave it for now. But I'd lie down if I were you.'

He began to walk slowly along the concrete corridor away from the flat. Then suddenly he stopped and turned. The net curtain had been pulled aside and for a split second he saw the woman's face. Her right eye was swollen and almost closed. The skin around it was blue and yellow. There was a large lump on the cheekbone below the eye and this drew her mouth into a lopsided rictus grin.

The curtain dropped and all he could see was the frosted glass.

'Call yourself an enforcer,' Big Boy said. 'What you enforcin', man?'

'You know what enforcer means?' Jelly said, flexing a bicep that was big enough to block the view from a side window. 'Enforcin's a big word.'

'What we enforcin'? We sittin' in the cold in the morning.' He used the word 'morning' as though it was an arcane time period with which he was unfamiliar. 'We ain't enforcin'.'

The Trans Am was parked in Praed Street near Paddington Station. The morning was wintry.

'We enforcin' for Goater. Maybe it don't seem like it, but enforcin' have many meanings; many ways of bein' enforced.'

'Jesus. Listen, why we don't go in? I mean we been here for hours. Who's to say he comin'?'

'Goater say we don't go in, OK?'

Big Boy brooded about this for some moments before saying, 'You know something? I don't give a shit what Goater say. I mean who he think he is with that fake collar? Yes, your reverend! Thank you, your reverend!'

'Don't let him fool you. Goater knows things. He got better contacts than anybody. I ain't going against him.'

'Chicken shit. Who he got to be heavy for him?'

'Us. That's who. We're heavy for him. We his enforcers and . . .' He paused and then said, 'Bingo!'

A cab had stopped on a double yellow line and a man in his thirties got out and entered a small office building. He was dressed in designer jeans and what looked to the boys like a very expensive soft brown leather jacket.

'He going to make the car,' Big Boy said. 'Get a cab.'

'Who going to pay for it?'

'Your pal Goater. He going to pay.'

Jelly said, 'Well . . . I mean . . .'

'He a reverend, ain't he?'

Jelly hailed a cab as one came out of the station. There were now three vehicles, two cabs and the Trans Am, waiting.

The man came out of the building with letters

in his hand. He got into his cab. It drove to the Bayswater Road, and there it turned west. Just ahead of it was the Trans Am, and just behind it was Jelly in the black cab.

Leo Silver drove along the Thames Embankment to Cannon Row. This time he was not moved by the beauty of the view downstream to Tower Bridge. He saw instead a light rain falling on the newly cleaned buildings making them look colder and wetter than their grimy counterparts.

Nor was he feeling at his best. The ambivalent reactions of the evening were still with him and he had slept feverishly and too long. Zoe was already gone by the time he woke but she left something for him.

On the bathroom door was a blown-up photocopy of a Thurber cartoon which showed a man and a woman in a room, the one saying to the other, 'Well, who made the magic go out of our marriage – you or me?'

In the original the man was asking the question but Zoe had changed the picture in such a way that the question now came from the woman.

At any other time he would have been amused. Not today.

He parked his dented Golf and went into the station. The desk sergeant said, 'The chief super wants you and your guv'nor as soon as he gets in.

Oh, and there was a call from someone called Coker and another from your girlfriend.'

'For Christ's sake, belt up!' Leo said.

The desk sergeant flinched. The tone had been savage and he had never heard that before from Leo Silver.

Leo went to his desk and phoned Laura.

'Hi,' she said.

'Hi.'

There was a pause.

'You OK?' she said.

'I'm fine. And you?'

'I'm fine. You sound—'

'I've got a meeting.'

'I just wanted to say hello.'

Her voice was warm, affectionate. He was irritated with himself for his lack of grace.

'I'm glad,' he said. 'I wanted to say hello too.'

'And I was wondering.'

'About what?'

'What you think now you've read it.'

'I haven't finished it.'

'Oh.'

Again he felt as though he had let her down.

'But I read quite a bit last night.'

'How far did you get?'

He told her and she said, 'The real stuff is still to come.'

'I gathered that.'

'When will I see you? Tonight?'

Leo saw Macrae stride past the open-plan office on his way to Wilson's room and hastily said, 'Look, I've got to go. I'll call you.' He put down the phone and hurried after Macrae.

Wilson was polishing his black shoes. He did this as he had once polished his black police boots. It gave him simple organic pleasure.

'Good morning, gentlemen.' He gave his shoes a last flick before putting the cleaning equipment into his bottom drawer. 'Ever been to Madeira?'

'I thought you'd decided on Florida?' Macrae said.

'Beryl now thinks we'll get shot before we leave the airport.'

'Zimmer frames,' Leo said.

'What?'

'In Madeira.'

'You been there?'

'No, sir, but it's a bit on the elderly side, isn't it?' Then he said quickly, 'I mean for someone like yourself, sir.'

Wilson looked sharply at him. 'That's what I think too. Anyway it's not why I wanted to see you.' He up-ended a large manila envelope on to his desk. It contained several pieces of paper of various sizes all neatly encased in protective plastic.

'From Forensic.' He stirred the contents with his fingers. 'This was the one found in the lavatory, the one that was caught under the seat.'

'Anything on it?' Macrae said.

'Not much, but they certainly found impressions.'

He looked at the form accompanying the evidence. 'They say they can identify an *M* and an *I*. Then the writing deteriorates. Then there's a line going up. Then it stops.'

'Maybe she died then,' Leo said.

Wilson said, 'It's possible. What's-his-name, the pathologist, said she died of suffocation. So it might have been like that. First the *M* then the *I* then a kind of scratching. I mean you can imagine what the hell happened. She was trying to write and she was dying at the same time.'

Leo said, 'Was the line going up obliquely as though to start a new letter?'

Wilson nodded.

'*Mi* . . .' Leo said. 'The new letter could have been an *L*. Mile? Milk?'

'For Christ's sake,' Macrae said. 'It could be any bloody thing. What else, Les?'

'He's given us a report on the hairs found on the sheet. Pubic mostly. A lot of them her own but a lot not.'

'Aye, he said something about that at the time.'

'He says some come from a wig. But no wig was found there.'

Leo said, 'I thought men took their toupées off before they embarked on—'

'Don't be coarse,' Macrae said.

'These were from an inexpensive wig,' Wilson said. 'I don't know who the hell this pathologist is but he's full of little bits and pieces of information.'

'I know him,' Macrae said. 'He's good.'

'He says there are three sorts of wigs. Man-made fibres the cheapest. Then wigs made from Asian hair and dyed. Also relatively cheap compared with wigs made from European hair and not dyed. Apparently there are enough shades in European hair so you don't have to dye it.'

'And this is?' Macrae said.

'He says it's Asian.'

Leo said, 'Why couldn't it just be from an Asian man who was getting his leg over?'

'That's a point, Les,' Macrae said, 'even if it was crudely put.'

'Because it was dyed and because the pathologist says he can tell it had been knotted into a wig-base. OK?'

They talked for another half hour then the meeting broke up. Macrae said to Leo, 'I've got to make a quick phone call then I want to go back to the girl's flat. You wait in the car.'

He went into his office, consulted his black book then dialled.

A woman's voice said, 'Yes?'

'Mrs Loftus, please.'

'Who the fuck're you?'

'I want—'

'Never mind what you want, you sod! How did you get this number, you shit, you bastard!'

There was a click and then another woman's voice said, 'Hello, who is this?'

Macrae said, 'Marge? It's George Macrae.'

'Oh, hello, George. Sorry about that but she came into the refuge a week ago and she's just beginning to get her confidence back.'

'No problem. I think I've got one for you. Whether she'll leave home is another matter.'

'Husband?'

'I'd bet on it. And he's a copper. There is one way. She's got a little girl of school age who isn't going to school, or wasn't this morning anyway. You could always say you were going to put the kid in care if she doesn't co-operate.'

'You saw her, then?'

'Just a glance. Face all damaged. Scared as hell. Bloody great chain on the door.'

'That never works,' Marge Loftus said. 'He says open up and she opens up. Too scared not to. But give me the address and I'll have a go.'

Chapter Sixteen

'You're sitting in the Captain's place,' the voice said. 'That's where the Captain sits.'

Naked Diary. That's the truth. That's how it happened. That's how I met Martin Kendrick. Those were his exact words— You're sitting in the Captain's place.

Jane and I were sitting at the big communal table having a beer. The table where we'd been told to sit if we wanted food. There was a leaf screen to keep off the sun and the wind but otherwise it was just out there between the bungalows and the sea. And we were the only guests at the place. Or at least that's what we had thought until I looked up and saw this man.

He was medium height and wearing a kind of sarong and a bush hat and holding this animal, this teddy bear, in his arms. It was an ordinary brown teddy bear with a kind of bandage round its head as though it had been in the wars.

'You want a beer?' he said to the bear. 'OK, we'll have a beer.' He ordered one from the son of the owner and stood there waiting for me to move. Then he said,

'The Captain is a person of habits. He likes to do things by the book.'

He was smiling and the bear's face had a kind of smile, and I thought how terrific this was and I moved along the bench and he sat down with the Captain and introduced himself and we had a beer together.

I mean it really was terrific. If you have a fantasy about your holidays in exotic places then this is part of it: the good-looking guy who comes out of nowhere and is able to make you smile and keep you interested.

Because that's what he did.

He'd been at the Waterfall Bungalows for a couple of days and he'd sussed out everything in Ban Khai and he and the Captain knew where to go and what to do.

He did a lot of his talking to the Captain and he'd say things to us like, 'The Captain would like to know if you would be his guest . . .' or 'The Captain wonders if . . .' and he'd be asking Jane and me to go with them on a jaunt.

That was another one of the Captain's words – jaunt.

There wasn't a hell of a lot to do in Ban Khai. I mean it's a small island and there are few roads. But the waterfalls: they were something else.

Martin and the Captain took us to see the waterfalls.

'The Captain loves waterfalls,' Martin said. 'He loves the noise they make.'

And he took us to the temples called Wats. The one nearest to the Waterfall Bungalows holds ten-day retreats for Westerners who want to meditate with the Buddhists but we only went to look.

'The Captain is C. of E.,' Martin said. 'I wouldn't want to embarrass him.'

Another time he took us out into the jungle. We hired mopeds and left the road and drove on small tracks and there were signs about being careful of cobras and scorpions and everything felt heavy and dense and unlike the jungles you see on the movies. This was real.

'The Captain fought the Japanese in a place like this, didn't you, old man?'

Whenever Martin spoke to the bear he always looked at it with interested eyes as though it really was alive and taking part in the conversation. He touched the old piece of bandage which was sewn on to its head. 'Shrapnel wound,' he said.

All these quotes are from Naked Diary so they're true.

The Naked Diary also has the real stuff about sex between Martin and me but I'm going to tone that down because this is supposed to be a Journal now and not so naked.

But there are one or two things from the diary that are interesting. The first is that Jane and I talked about Martin. Not a long talk but enough for me to know I wasn't harming her in any way. 'I'm bruised,' she said, meaning from her boyfriend leaving her and going on to Bali. She said she wouldn't have taken Martin on even if I wasn't there.

That made the difference.

*The other thing was this. We used to have sex after
we smoked grass – you can buy it anywhere in Thailand
even from kids. Sometimes we made love down by the
sea at night sometimes up in his bungalow. But he
always had the bear with him and he would turn him
away from us so he was looking in another direction
and he would say—*

Leo saw Macrae coming and hastily put the Journal
on the back seat.

They drove in the direction of Lancaster Gate.
After a few moments Macrae said, 'D'you know a
DS called Lightly?'

'Vice Squad?'

'Aye.'

'I've seen him around.'

Macrae grunted, sat back, and began to read the
Daily Telegraph.

Leo found a parking space behind Sebastopol
Mansions and he and Macrae went up in the lift.
The police tapes were on the door but there was
activity inside the apartment and they had hardly
crossed the threshold when Tompkins said to Leo,
'A Mr Coker phoned. Says he's been trying to get in
touch with you.'

'Who's that?' Macrae said.

'The chiropodist, guv'nor. He left a message to
phone him. I was waiting to get here.'

As Leo went into another room to phone, Macrae

went into the bedroom and looked at the bedhead. There were still a number of hairs on it. Why a wig? Who went to bed in a wig, especially for sex?

Leo came back.

'What did he want?' Macrae said.

'First he wanted to know if I could steer any colleagues to him.'

'What the hell for?'

'Says police have bad feet and—'

'For Christ's sake, is that all?'

'One other thing. He says the priest he saw coming out of here was black.'

'Black? Why the hell didn't he tell us that to start with?'

'Says he got confused by our questioning.'

'Doesn't make much difference. There're hundreds of black clergymen in Britain these days. We still don't know who the hell he was.'

'I was wondering, guv'nor . . .'

'Wondering? Does Zoe know about that?'

Leo let it pass. 'Wondering about black clergymen . . . you know that pimp you've used in the past as an informer?'

'What pimp?'

'The one with the rustic name. Something like—'

'Jesus Christ!' It was almost a shout. 'And with a woman! And coming out of the apartment of a tart!' He stood rubbing his bald head. 'I wonder . . .'

*

The buffalo carrying lead stood in the doorway of Lysander Goater's apartment making the place look small and vulnerable.

'Good morning, Mr Macrae,' Goater said. 'Oh, and Sergeant Silver. My lucky day.'

'We'll see about that,' Macrae said. 'Unless I am very much mistaken, Lysander, I suspect that you and I have something to discuss.'

'What would that be?'

'The death of a woman called Julia Maddox by violent means in a flat in Lancaster Gate, and the fact that you were seen coming out of that flat on the day she was murdered.'

Leo wasn't sure he had ever heard Macrae lie as much as he had in the past couple of days.

'Am I to understand that you have a positive ID on me?'

'I'm going to tell you something, Lysander. A witness described a small black clergyman. By his side was a tall attractive young woman. In the flat was a dead young woman who we think was on the game. I ask myself who of the many hundreds of black clergymen in Britain would this man resemble and I come up with you. My sergeant agrees with me.'

'Mr Macrae, I don't think—'

'But that's just for the lawyers who like that sort of thing. As far as I'm concerned, if you go on denying it and not wishing to discuss it, I'm going to arrest you for being an illegal immigrant.'

'An illegal immigrant?' Goater was outraged. 'My lawyers would laugh you out of court.'

'A man who pretends to be a clergyman could as easily be lying about his nationality and it might take weeks in a holding cell before he could prove it to our satisfaction.'

Goater indicated a couple of chairs. 'I thought this would happen. And it's so unfair.'

'You're not looking for justice, are you?' Macrae said.

'Not from the Metropolitan Police, that's for sure.'

'Sergeant, take a note of that, would you? Head it Statements made by the Witness to the Derogation of the Police Service.'

Goater held his hand up. 'Would a coffee get me off?'

'Coffee and information,' Macrae said.

They had coffee and Leo took notes and then Macrae said, 'OK, Lysander, let's see what we've got. You and this young woman – what's her name?'

'She's no one. Believe me.'

'Bullshit. She's a witness.'

'I'll make a deal with you – and I've got a lot to deal with.'

'You'd better have. You're the number one suspect in a nasty killing. I don't know why we just don't take you in now and charge you.'

'Two reasons. Firstly, you know me and you don't believe in your heart of hearts, if such an organ exists, that I had anything to do with this killing and' – he held up his hand to silence Macrae – 'and secondly, if you did that the real killer would get off and I think I can put you on to him.'

Macrae leaned back. 'Why?' he said.

'Why what?'

'Why would *you* know what I believe?'

'Not because I'm psychic but because I know you. When I read you were on the case I said to . . . to myself that if the witness described me it would take you ten seconds to come up with my name.'

'Two seconds.'

Leo waited in vain to hear credit given where it was due.

Goater went on, 'And I thought that I had better, for my own sake, find out what really happened.'

He told them what the boys had discovered.

'Michael Knight?' Macrae said to Leo. 'Mean anything to you?'

Leo shook his head. 'I'll check with the Drugs boys.'

Goater said, 'All I could get at first was the name Mike or Mikey. But then the boys followed him to his pad in Castlenau. And it's some pad, a big house near the river.'

He gave them the address of the house and an office in Paddington then Macrae said, 'OK, the woman's name.'

'We had a deal,' Goater said.

Macrae smiled without warmth. 'I'll tell you what your deal's worth, Lysander. Sergeant ·Silver and I

177

are going to do some checking and if anything is different from what you say we're coming back. And God help you – and the girl.'

'Oh, Lightly! The very man.'

Lightly was coming into the station. He stopped and turned.

'How about a drink?' Macrae said.

Lightly's face, with the Zapata moustache turning down the sides of his mouth, was set in its permanent scowl.

'It's all right,' Macrae said. 'It's after five and I won't tell anyone.'

Lightly rearranged his face. 'That's a good idea, sir.'

They went across to the Red Lion. Macrae waited and Lightly said, 'What'll you have, sir?'

'Large Glenmorangie and a pint of heavy.'

The Vice Squad detective blinked, then said, 'Coming up.'

They took their drinks to a table. The pub was empty at this time of the afternoon.

'I've been doing my homework,' Macrae said.

'How's that, sir?'

'Checking on what you told me. And it's true. I mean, you haven't exaggerated in the least.'

Lightly rearranged his face once more and tried to give it an interested and alert expression.

'You've done well in the written papers, no doubt

about that. The question is: what happens at the interviews.'

'That's what I mean, sir.'

'I'll tell you. We're all detectives, and we all have bits and pieces of information about each other. So when a detective comes up before a group of other detectives, they put these little bits together. It's like a case, Lightly.'

Lightly's expression began to slip. Macrae kept up the light ironic tone.

'When the Board has put them together a picture emerges. And in this case, you're at the centre of it.'

'I don't follow . . . sir.'

'That's why I'm here. To help you understand. You see, Lightly, you're on Vice and you can't help but come into contact with vice. Nothing else would make sense. Right?'

'Right, sir.'

'And vice mostly means tarts. Now the bits of information about you indicate that you deal with the tarts rather harshly.'

'They're the enemy, sir.'

'By God, laddie, I wish I'd said that! The enemy. That's how you feel, is it?'

'That's how I feel.'

'And you treat them like the enemy? With all that implies?'

Lightly said nothing.

'The problem, laddie, is that you're a very big

man, and you've got a very hot temper. And what you do is not allowed, Lightly. Not allowed at all.'

'It's not true, sir.'

'What isn't?'

'I know what you're getting at. There were a couple of accusations—'

'Four.'

'You know as well as I do, sir, that they'll say anything. Not a shred of proof.'

'That's what I was getting to. You see, there might have been something I could have done for you. I could have gone to a couple of pals and said Lightly deserves a better grade than sergeant. And when they brought up the accusations I could have said a man is innocent until proved guilty. That's how we operate, isn't it, laddie?'

Lightly's face was drawn and tight. 'Yes, sir.'

'But then I had a problem. I'm going to explain it to you. And I'm also going to let you into something. The way forward in the police depends on many things and one of the most important is a good family background.' As he said it Macrae had the grace to flinch inwardly.

'Wives are important these days. In politics. In business. But specially in the police. What we want in the Met are wives who can mix with anyone, and who can support their men; what we don't want are wives that keep the shutters up and the curtains drawn. Wives who can't show their faces because their faces are too terrible to look at.'

Macrae paused and drank some of his malt whisky. 'Nothing like a dram,' he said.

Lightly kept silent. His eyes were wary.

'You know what I mean?' Macrae said. 'Sometimes the wives get so frightened they lose touch with reality. But there are organizations now that can help them.' He rose. 'Thanks for the drink, Lightly. Oh, remember me to your wife. And I'll remember you to Frenchy.'

He turned and left.

Chapter Seventeen

Zoe was at an advertising dinner in Soho and Leo had gone to his parents for an early supper after an anguished phone call from his mother. He had walked into a major row. It was his father's chess club night yet Manfred was sitting on the sofa in the living-room pretending to read *Grove's Dictionary of Music*. Since no one Leo knew had ever read *Grove* for pleasure – not the 1948 edition, anyway – he assumed that something major had occurred.

His mother was seated at the big table on which there was her sewing machine. It was idle.

'I said to your father, "You go to chess you don't have wife (*vife*) no more," ' Lotte said. Her face was flushed and her hair more than usually awry. 'He don't talk to me,' she said to Leo. Then she turned to the sofa and hissed, 'Macho Man!'

Manfred continued reading about the early life of Beethoven.

'You know what he done?' Lotte said. Leo realized from her lapses in grammar how serious the situation was. 'He buys a duvet. He doesn't tell me. Not a word (*vurd*). And a duvet cover. Oh, yes, everything. Complete. A set. God knows how much.'

Manfred turned over a page, put his finger on the text, and said, 'Who had a new kitchen?'

'My own money! Not ours.'

'Your money is always your money,' Manfred said. 'How come my money is our money?'

'Look, if this is just going to be a straight "domestic", I'm off,' Leo said.

'What is "domestic"?' Lotte said.

'What the police call rows in families. And we don't like to get embroiled.'

'I'd like to embroil your father on a hot stove.'

'Broil!' Manfred said. 'Why can't you speak English?'

Lotte made a gesture with her hands as though to banish and embroil him at the same time.

'Our bedroom is green,' she said. 'Your father buys a duvet with a *blue* cover. So who made new curtains?'

'They were old,' Manfred said.

'Old but good. And with new curtains the walls looked so bad. Grimy, you know. So—'

'My God,' Leo said. 'Don't tell me.'

'Yes,' his mother said. 'We had them painted.'

'You said they needed it,' Manfred said.

'But . . . BUT . . .' Lotte began, her voice rising, 'my darling, you have not heard the end of the story.'

Manfred hurriedly returned to *Grove*.

'One night!' Lotte said. 'The duvet lasts one night. Why? It is too hot, that is why.'

'Because of tog,' Manfred said. 'And you know what your mother said? Your mother who knows everything about bedrooms and bathrooms and . . . other places. She says, "Tog? Tog? What is tog?" '

'You only knew because you went to the shop!'

'I am a musician. I am not supposed to know such things.'

'What is tog?' Leo said.

His father said, 'It is the number to tell you how hot the duvet is. I took it back and said you must give me one with a lower tog and they said, "Have you slept in this?" So what must I say? I tell the truth and they say so sorry.'

Lotte said to Leo, 'What is it in a car that tells the engine how hot it is?'

'A thermostat.'

'That is what your father needs. A proper thermostat.' She shrugged. 'You're going to pay me, Manfy. The material. The painting. That's a lot of money.'

Manfred turned to his son. 'These are not like duvets from the old days. In Vienna we had no tog.'

'And you know what now?' Lotte said. 'Your father doesn't have the duvet no longer.'

'Any longer,' Manfred said.

She ignored him. 'But . . . *but* . . . now he wants his aircell blankets in the duvet cover! Are you hearing me, darling? Aircell blankets in a duvet cover.'

'How're you going to keep them from rumpling up?' Leo said.

'Aaah,' Lotte said. 'Such a clever boy. If he had a clever father this would not have happened.'

Leo got home about nine feeling, as he often felt after a visit to his parents, exasperated. This was replaced by an unease which he soon diagnosed: he had to finish reading the Journal. He fetched it from the car and ran a bath. He lowered himself into the water and began to read.

You think you KNOW.

If you could write it the way you want to write it you could say: I knew, I guessed . . .

He paused. He didn't really want to read Samantha's story. It focused his mind on things he didn't want to focus on. To paraphrase Zoe, he was not exactly the Leo Silver that he himself knew and loved.

The pride and elation he had felt at bedding an attractive woman like Laura had disappeared. So too, but not completely, the guilt. He had told himself that things like that happened, especially in police work. But it had scared the wits out of him, for looking down that long and tortuous road into the future, he had descried the ghostly figure of his guv'nor, and the one person Leo did not want to become was a second George Macrae, with his two ex-wives and a mistress who would probably also leave him in the end.

But he would only become like Macrae if Zoe found out what had happened – and she was not going to find out.

He would finish the Journal and send it back to Laura. Then his life would revert to normal.

But he had, willy-nilly, become involved with Samantha and, with a sinking heart, knew that he was going to become even more involved as she fell through the bottom of her world.

He didn't want to become involved. He wanted her to go away. And he wanted Laura to go away. There had been another phone call from her that day. He was sick and tired of the knowing look in the desk sergeant's eyes as he passed on her messages.

In fact she was becoming something of a liability. Yet he knew that if something equally bad happened to a member of his own family – including Ruth – he would pull out all the stops even if it meant involving strangers.

He turned his attention to the Journal once more. Finish it, he told himself. Then finish with the whole goddam business.

You think you KNOW.

If you could write it the way you want to write it you could say: I knew. I guessed.

That way you wouldn't seem such a bloody fool.

But Naked Diary says no you bloody didn't know . . .
So get on with it.

'The Captain says all good things come to an end.'

We were on the beach watching the fireflies, Jane had left the night before and we'd had one long day to ourselves.

I knew that what the Captain said was right but I also knew something the Captain didn't know. That it wasn't the end, but only the beginning.

What now?

Martin was a Londoner, so was I. Martin had left university without a job; so had I. Martin wanted to see the world before he settled down; so did I. Both of us wanted the same things.

'The Captain says this is what happens to people when they meet on holiday in foreign parts. He says they fall in love but it doesn't last.'

I said, 'Is that how you feel? Is this just a holiday affair?'

And he said, 'You heard what the Captain thought. It's not necessarily what I think.'

Those are direct quotes from Naked Diary.

I wanted him to say something more, but he didn't. And I thought: Don't push your luck.

We left the following evening. The bus ride was sweaty and hot like it had been coming, but he was sitting next to me and I didn't care.

I remember it well. He sat with the Captain on his lap, his eyes closed, his face like a mask.

I should have known then.

But you never do.

Christ, that day was hectic. I was leaving on the ten o'clock flight that night, Martin two days later. We had everything to do. Money. Check tickets. Check seat on plane. Buy presents. And we only arrived in Bangkok at dawn.

Even so we saw each other. Had time together. He rented a room and we made love and then we washed each other very gently under the shower.

The time came to get to the airport. We sat in the departure lounge and Martin had the Captain on his lap but he wasn't talking too much though his fingers were fretting at the bandage.

Then he said, 'I want you to have him.'

'Who?'

'The Captain.'

'But you love him,' I said.

'I love you too. I want you to have him.'

He undid my pack and put in the Captain.

I almost cried. 'I'll look after him,' I said.

'I know you will.'

'Will you visit him in London?'

'Of course. My two favourite people.' Then he stood up. 'I'll get some cigarettes.'

'I've got some.'

'I need some.'

I watched him go over to the counter at the far end. A small Thai man in grey trousers and a white shirt stopped him and they talked for a moment.

Then a voice right at my ear said, 'Quickly. Come with me.'

I looked round. It was Jane.

'I thought you'd gone.'

*She grabbed my pack. 'For God's sake,' she said.
'You're in terrible danger.'*

'Why? What's—?'

'Come on. I'll explain.'

Her thin face was drawn, her eyes were hot.

That's from Naked Diary so it must be true.

*She hurried me into the ladies' washroom. There
were a couple of women there but she pushed me into
a cubicle and shut the door.*

'What the hell's going on?' I said.

*She wasn't listening. She undid the top of my pack
and took out the Captain. Then she did something
awful. She pulled off his head.*

'No!' I cried.

'Look!'

I saw the plastic bags.

'Oh, Christ!'

She fished one out and tore it open. White powder.

'You think I can't spot guys like Martin?' she said.

*She poured the powder into the toilet bowl until it
had all gone. Then she flushed it and said, 'You were
just a mule.'*

Naked Diary goes a bit mad here. You've got to think
how I was feeling. We all know about drug smuggling
in Thailand. They've got the fucking death sentence.
And if you don't get that, it's years and years.

'When did you know?' I said.

'I didn't know, not for sure. But something like it

happened to me once. I couldn't say anything at Ban Khai. I mean you were too involved. But I thought, if he tries it anywhere he'll try it at the airport when you're leaving.'

The heroin was still scumming the lavatory bowl and she flushed again.

She said, 'You go to the door. See if you can see him. Then we'll get you to the boarding queue another way. I'll bring the pack.'

I went to the door and looked out. He was on the bench where we'd been sitting, but he had his back to me.

'It's OK,' I called. 'He can't see us.'

'Right,' Jane said. 'Here's the pack. You get going.'

He just sat there smoking and we went round the lounge without him seeing us.

I followed the departure signs and Jane came after me. We reached a queue. I grabbed my pack from her.

'Oh, God, I'm so grateful,' I said.

We put our arms around each other and hugged. She said she'd see me in London. The queue moved forward. I came to the top of it and a small Thai man in grey slacks and a white shirt said, 'Goo-day. Come wi' me please.'

He and another man and a woman took me to a room and they opened my pack and on the top were two big boxes of chocolates.

'You li' sweet things?' he said.

'No, I—' and then I realized Jane must have given them to me and I said, 'Yeah. I like chocolates.'

But of course there were no chocolates. No choc-olates at all. This was the real stuff, not the bloody talc we'd flushed down the lavatory.

Several pages had been torn out of the Journal at this point and Leo noticed there were marks on the paper as though Samantha had tried to scratch out some of the lines first.

Now it changed from a neatly typed manuscript to a collection of pages on to which pieces of typed or handwritten paper had been glued. He guessed that these might have been cut or torn from the original Naked Diary and he was partly right. Some, according to a note by Samantha, were from the Diary which had been written on scraps of paper in Bangkok gaol where no such writing was allowed. She had written it at night and eventually smuggled it out.

Later she had made an effort, either in Puckle-hurst, the women's prison in England, or even after she had been released, to produce a coherent narra-tive. He began to wonder if he wasn't reading the first draft of a manuscript, still rough, in which Laura's sister hoped eventually to interest a publisher.

He read on:

You looking for a sting? This was perfect. I mean so bloody perfect it wasn't till I was shoved in gaol that I knew. And then I had to be told by Barbie.

　　Barbie . . . Barbie . . . you saved my life, kid.

　　Ai . . . ki . . . do . . . baby.

　　You know sometimes I can't remember how you look. But I can hear your voice. Feel your hands. Sense your love . . .

Five in a cell. We're in the Third World. You sit in the airport and believe it is First World. Better than London. Better than Amsterdam. Here it's Third World.

You think women are clean? Christ. Women are filthy . . . filthy . . .

Barbie, you were so right, baby. I remember your voice. Those long vowels; that nasal Aussie drawl. I've never been there. Oh, Barbie . . . I owe you more than my life . . . Remember when you found me with that Greek woman and the two Korean dykes . . . They would have done me then . . . Female rape . . . Christ, I'd only barely heard there was such a thing . . .

　　Ai

　　Ki

　　Do . . . baby . . .

　　Harmony . . . Energy . . . The Way . . .

　There's you in everything.

*

There was evidence of more scratchings out and torn pages and Leo flipped on. His bath-water was getting cold but he knew Zoe would be coming back soon and he wanted to be rid of this awful Journal.

He skimmed descriptions of the gaol. The Bangkok female prison sounded worse than the worst male prisons he had been to in England.

Barbie told me what had happened. She knew. She was in for drugs. It had nearly happened to her. The Thai Drugs Squad gets twenty-five per cent of the value of the drugs impounded. I was charged with twenty-one kilos. Think about it. A kilo is over two pounds. That's more than forty pounds weight of heroin. I could have bought the Drugs Squad for that. You can see why they load the weight. Twenty-five per cent of more than twenty kilos is real money.

But why had Martin and Jane done it like that?
That took longer to find out and I'm not dead sure even now. Almost sure but not absolutely. But one day I'll be absolutely, absolutely sure.

More scratchings out, then:

Think about it. Think about who's gone to gaol in Bang-

kok. *The big boys? Bullshit. People like me, and some a lot dimmer.*

Oh, Barbie, if it hadn't been for you, baby.

When you left I nearly died – of sorrow. But I lived because of what you had taught me. Not only physically but mentally.

Plead guilty, you said.

What? What? What?

Plead guilty. You'll never get a decent lawyer out here and if you plead guilty there's a chance of the King's pardon. You make them work at you, you embarrass them about twenty kilos and they get tough because they have to hide their lies.

So plead guilty.

And I did.

And the King's pardon? Yeah, it worked. But only in part. Twenty years they gave me. And I served four. Then they sent me back to England and I did two more in Pucklehurst.

That was a doddle.

You want to read more? You want to read about Puckle—

*

'Are you alive in there?' Zoe's voice called.

'I'm coming out now,' Leo said.

He closed the Journal and hid it under his dressing-gown on the floor.

He opened the bathroom door and stood dripping and naked, experiencing a feeling of love, gratitude and lust.

'I didn't make the magic go out of our marriage,' he said. 'Get into bed and I'll prove it.'

'Talk . . . talk . . . talk . . !' Zoe said, kicking off her shoes.

Chapter Eighteen

At about the time Leo was emerging from the bathroom, Macrae was standing at the window of his office in Cannon Row. It was a meagre room with only a partial view of the river but even so it was a good deal better than his home, with its dirty dishes and unmade empty bed, which was why he hadn't left yet.

Sometimes he despaired of himself. Was it always going to be like this? And if not, what the hell *was* it going to be like?

Les Wilson had told him often enough that by now he should have been a chief superintendent, perhaps even a deputy commander. And Wilson frequently made the point that Macrae was his own worst enemy.

So be it. But what would he have had to do to get ahead? If Scales was the paradigm then committees, paperwork, training courses, after-dinner speeches . . . those were the ways ahead.

Well, they could go and fuck themselves as far as he was concerned. He was, and always had been, a thief-taker. His background was the Flying Squad in the great days. He wasn't some nearlyman, some bloody paper pusher, some twat who thought the villains were more important than their victims.

So what *did* he want?

More money for a start. That would help. What else? Foreign holidays? He wasn't too keen on foreigners or foreign food – except curry. There were always women. But he didn't want women plural. At the moment he wanted woman singular.

He wanted Frenchy.

He and Frenchy had an undiscussed working arrangement. She had a life, he had a life, and unless he was going to offer her something – riches? glamour? the privilege of being the third Mrs Macrae? – what she did with her own life was not his business. When she said she was going to see her mother it was her business and he asked no questions.

Enter Detective Sergeant Lightly, a shit of the first order and a violent one at that, and things had changed.

He dialled the computer room.

'Colley here.'

'Neil, it's George Macrae.'

'Listen, we've got the print-out you asked for on the Bayswater thing.'

'Fine. There's something else. I want the address and number of a Mrs Pinker. I'm pretty sure her phone's ex-directory and she may even have some form, she was married to some right villains.'

He had hardly put the receiver down when the phone rang.

'George, this is Marge Loftus.'

'Did you get her?'

'Yes and no. I mean she's here, at the refuge, but God knows if she'll stay.'

'I should have thought once you got her there it would have been a piece of cake.'

'That's what everyone thinks, but battered wives aren't like that. At least some of them aren't. There's a psychological term for it but what it means—'

'I can understand words of more than one syllable.'

'Sorry. I didn't want to sound pretentious. The syndrome is called affiliation by fear and it means that if you've been beaten up and abused as much as she has it's possible you begin to associate peace and what passes for brief happiness as belonging to the period *after* you've experienced the violence. So subconsciously you look for the violence to give you the peace. It's Pavlovian. You with me?'

'You mean it's like banging your head against a brick wall because it's nice when you stop?'

'More or less.'

'Have you got the kid too?'

'Yes. She's with her mother. There are half a dozen other kids here and with any luck she'll get used to them and get used to being a child again. But it will take a long time and mightn't work anyway.'

'Did you have to threaten Mrs Lightly with the social service?'

'I'm afraid so. Which means the two of them are as close as limpets.'

'Marge, please keep me posted. I've got the husband running around the station trying to become an important copper.'

Frensham Street near the Elephant and Castle was like a thousand other streets in South London, with rows of terraced houses, some decorated with little privet hedges, some with potted plants and some with front gardens of tarmac where the owners parked their cars.

Macrae pulled up at number seventeen (two bay trees in concrete tubs). He knew it was late. He knew he should not be doing this, but things had changed.

He rang the doorbell and heard the unmistakable sound of chimes.

He had gone through phases of intense jealousy and intense anger. These had produced the worst heart fibrillation he had yet experienced and he had become frightened. Even though he was feeling no obvious heart pains he still remembered what Bulloch had said: you'd better be in intensive care in ten minutes, otherwise . . . so he had to banish the jealousy and anger, not an easy thing when his mind was producing clear images of that bastard Lightly in bed with Frenchy.

But he knew he had a bigger problem than visualizing a Vice Squad sergeant having a bit of rumpo.

It was something that had clearly been growing in the past few months and had now been triggered: the thing was, he didn't want Frenchy having it off with *anyone* other than himself.

And so he was not standing there with a metaphorical stick in his hand ready to beat her, he was—

'Yes?'

A woman's voice came from a small security microphone in the wall.

'Is Frenchy in?'

The wall said, 'You got a bloody nerve coming round at this time of night and asking for my daughter!'

'Is that Mrs Pinker?'

'Course it's Mrs Pinker, who'd you think it was?'

'It's George Macrae.'

'Who's that?'

'George Macrae, Frenchy's friend.'

'The copper?'

'Aye. The copper.'

'Well, why didn't you say so?'

The door opened and he stepped into a small passageway. Mrs Pinker, in a gold dressing-gown, was standing at the bottom of the stairs. She had a cigarette in one corner of her mouth and was using her hands to place a white wig on her head.

'Sorry to be so late,' Macrae said.

She managed to settle the wig, then, with eyes half closed against the smoke, studied him for a moment and said, 'You don't look like a Capricorn.'

'Mum?' Frenchy's voice came from upstairs. 'You OK?'

'It's your boyfriend.' Mrs Pinker turned back to him and said, 'You can see her in the sitting-room. You're not going upstairs. I'm not having any of that, you understand me?'

'Absolutely,' Macrae said.

He stood in the front room with its overstuffed chairs and the table on which the planchette still stood. He hadn't been prepared for Mrs Pinker but if he asked himself what elderly women who had been associated with villains were like, he would have to say they were often like her: women whose early habits of good behaviour settled back on them like dust in later life.

'George?'

Frenchy stood in the doorway. She had pulled on a pair of jeans and a white blouse and the breasts he knew so well were pointing at him like pneumatic pistols.

'What're you doing here?'

With his new attitude in mind and the additional advantage of resting his heart, he said, 'D'you mind if I sit down?'

'Please yourself.'

He sat, she stood.

'You're not pleased to see me,' he said.

'How did you get this address?'

'I'm a copper, we have ways.'

'I never said don't come here, but I never thought you would. This is *my* place.'

'I know that, but something's come up.'

'Something always comes up.'

He thought he had never seen her looking better, with her animal vitality and voluptuous good looks. If you had those, what more did you want?

'Believe me, I wouldn't have disturbed you except—'

'You've come to check up on me!'

'No, I haven't. I swear I haven't.'

She was really angry yet he sensed there was something besides the anger. He told himself to keep cool for she was looking – in her own territory – more than somewhat in charge and he realized he had never really talked with her in a home other than his own.

He told her briefly about DS Lightly and was surprised to see what he thought was momentary relief in her eyes.

'Never heard of him,' she said and he wanted to believe her.

'He said he'd seen you at the London Towers.'

'I don't care what he said.'

'Why would he have said it if I prove him a liar so easily?'

'So you *are* checking up on me?'

'I am in a way. I'm also here to warn you—'

'Warn me! Who the hell do you think you are, George? I'll come and go as I please. You don't own—'

'Not that! Not that at all! About *him*. He's looking for promotion and wants to use our – friendship to . . .'

'What? To blackmail you?'

'Sort of. The problem is he's a rough sod and I didn't want you, you know—'

She came into the room and put her arms round him. He pushed his face against her breasts.

'I've missed you,' he said in a muffled voice. 'Isn't there some place we can go? Like Battersea?'

'I been reading about the case you're on.'

'Don't change the subject.'

'When you going to finish it?'

'In a couple of days I hope. We know the bugger who did it. Or at least I think we do.'

He felt her exhale slowly. She felt soft and wonderfully familiar. He put his hand up and cupped her breast. She took his hand away.

'Not here, George.'

'Come home, then.'

'I'll think about it.'

When he was back in his car driving west he realized that they had not mentioned the word that had started all this: the word was money.

Chapter Nineteen

Leo drove to Battersea to pick up Macrae. He was happy for the first time in days. He had made love to Zoe the night before. It had been good, just like always, and they had slept folded around each other. When they woke they had made love again in the early morning.

So, OK. Back to normal. No more guilt.

He had finished the bloody Journal. And thank God for that. Now all he had to do was get it back to Laura, tell her he had spoken to the guys running the computer and that there was nothing on it about Martin Kendrick.

So it was a lie; so what?

The point was that he was leery of these people. Especially Samantha and Kendrick. As for Laura, it might have been fun, in other circumstances, to have had an affair with her. But . . . and it was a big but . . . some of the senior coppers who had gone down the tubes in recent years had gone down because of their friendship with people who weren't kosher – wealthy property developers, car dealers with form, or just plain villains.

He drew up a few yards from Macrae's house. From there he could see Macrae in the small sitting-room. He was standing in the middle of the room with his hand on his wrist as though taking his pulse – which Leo knew was nonsense.

They drove north across the river.

Macrae said, 'I got a print-out on this sod Knight. Let's go to Paddington and see if Goater's two donkeys have got it right.'

'How d'you think Goater got on to him, guv'nor?'

'He's got more contacts than all of us at Cannon Row put together. He was probably running Julia Maddox, or had been at one time, otherwise why the hell was he there?'

'What you said he was there for: to do her in.'

'Bullshit. Goater's not the type. But he was bloody scared we'd think he was; that's why he did his own investigation. He must have known she was on drugs. It was obvious. She was giving Takorides money to look the other way when her customers came in, and probably paying him to look the other way when her drugs were delivered. Goater might even have organized things for her. If we know about the pizzas you can bet that he did. I mean *he* could have been paying Takorides too.'

'And he thinks it's a drug-related murder but doesn't know who the supplier is so—'

'So he does our job for us, knowing that if he doesn't he might be a suspect. See? We get there a bit late but we get there.'

They crossed Hyde Park and made for Paddington Station. At this time in the morning traffic was heavy. Macrae unfolded a piece of listing paper and said, 'Michael (Mike) Knight . . . thirty-six . . . comes originally from Hereford . . . alias Roland Christie, Chris Roland . . . First arrested on drugs as a student growing marijuana in his mother's greenhouse. Cautioned . . . Lived in Spain for a time . . . He's got form in Europe too . . . Never been convicted . . . Nothing much at all.'

'You haven't given me the address, guv'nor.'

Macrae told him, then said, 'You remember what the time was when Goater said his boys had seen Knight?'

'Half-past ten, wasn't it? Stands to reason if it's a mail-drop he must come after the mail's been delivered.'

'Park over there. We're in good time.'

They parked on a double yellow line and settled down to wait.

Macrae said, 'You know anything about wigs?'

'Only what we heard from the pathologist.'

'I know men wear them.' He touched his bald head. 'What about women?'

'Old ones do when they start losing their hair.'

'What about younger ones? Does Zoe?'

'Never. Orthodox Jewish women do.'

Macrae did not reply.

They waited for more than two hours until well past eleven o'clock. During that time three traffic wardens tried to ticket them for illegal parking.

'This is getting a wee bit aggravating,' Macrae said. 'It's not as though we haven't got better things to do.'

'We could get a search warrant,' Leo said. 'Have a look at the place. Or we could go to his house in Hammersmith.'

'And what the hell do we say? "Excuse me, Mr Knight, but we think you've been a naughty boy"? Forget it. He'd never have anything at the house. This is where whatever's happening is happening.' He took out a slim panatella, unwrapped it then put it back in the packet. 'Oh, shit,' he said. 'Come on, let's take a look.'

As he spoke the car telephone buzzed and he picked it up. He identified himself and listened for half a minute. 'Oh, Christ!' he said. 'You still there? Aye, I'm on my way.'

He put the phone down, 'Something's come up. Not this case, something else. I've got to go. You watch for him. If he doesn't come soon, have a look around.'

'Guv'nor, what about—?'

But Macrae was out of the car before Leo could finish the sentence. A taxi coming out of the station stopped for him. Then he was gone.

'Shit!' Leo said.

Irritated, he sat on for another fifteen minutes then left the car and walked to the three-storey building. There was a hairdresser's on the ground floor.

He went up the stairs to the first floor where there were two office doors separated by a narrower one. The first had a notice announcing Gold Secretarial, the narrow door was blank and the third had a small handwritten card on it which said No. 5 and the word Letters, with an arrow pointing to a postal slot.

Leo tried the door but it was locked. He went up the stairs to the third floor but the doors were open and the rooms empty. He returned to Gold Secretarial, knocked and went in.

A tiny woman in late middle age who wore her glasses on a cord and had a 1959 bouffant hairstyle was at a desk, typing.

Leo held his warrant card out for her to look at and then said, 'Have you been here all morning?'

'Yes. Why?'

'We've had a report of a possible bomb at Paddington Station and we're searching the buildings.'

'Oh, my God! Are you from the . . . the . . .?'

'Bomb Squad. Have you had anyone in here this morning?'

'Nobody.'

'What about the room next door?'

'That's a store-room.'

'And the one beyond?'

'That's Mr Christie. He only comes for his mail, I think. He hasn't been this morning. I'd have seen him.'

'Could I look in the store-room?'

'Yes, of course.'

She unlocked the smaller door. The smell was unwholesome. 'It's where the mops and buckets are kept,' she said. 'Not that anyone cleans the building these days. This used to be a wash-room when the rooms on this floor were owned by one company.'

'OK, I'll have a look. You go back to your office.'

He switched on the light and closed the door. There were shelves which were empty but for old rags. A clutch of ancient mops and brooms stood in one corner. Behind the shelving unit were the wash-basin and lavatory. The basin was cracked and the lavatory had no seat, but once upon a time, as the lady from Gold Secretarial had said, this had been part of an office suite.

Leo walked further in. The room was narrow and he saw, at the far end, what he had hoped for: two other doors. They were let into the walls from the adjoining rooms so that access to the wash-room could be gained without going into the corridor.

The door into Gold Secretarial had been secured and he imagined that if he went into the office again he would see that the wall had been papered to hide the door. But the one on the other side, which led into No 5, was only bolted from the inside. He pushed back the bolt and pulled the door. It was stiff and almost immovable. He exerted all his strength and it opened with a scraping noise.

He found himself looking into an empty room with a window that was covered by a venetian blind. On the floor below the door was a pile of junk mail.

He stirred it with a foot but could see no name except The Occupier. Either Mr Knight had had no personal mail today or else Gold Secretarial had not seen him come to collect it.

He was turning back towards the store-room when he heard footsteps in the passage outside. The footsteps stopped and the letter flap opened and shut with a clang. A brown envelope came sailing through the air and landed on the floor. The postman? So late?

Leo grabbed the envelope and his stomach gave an uncomfortable heave. There was no stamp on it. On the left hand side and underlined were the words, By Hand. It was addressed to Martin Kendrick, Esq.

He ran back through the store-room. He could hear whoever had delivered the letter walking down the uncarpeted staircase which led to the street.

'Hey!' he shouted. 'Hang on a moment!'

The footsteps stopped. Leo belted down the stairs and saw a man standing at the door.

'Did you drop this into an office upstairs?' He held up the letter.

The man was in his thirties with short hair and a pale skin. His face was bony. He was wearing a sweat shirt and jeans under a tweed overcoat that looked of good quality.

'Did I do something wrong?'

'No.'

'Well, what're you—?'

'I was in the office when the letter landed.' Leo identified himself.

'A copper? Why? What's going on?'

'We're interested in Mr Kendrick. Come back inside for a moment.'

The two stood in the small entrance hall on the ground floor.

'How d'you mean, interested?'

'Just interested.'

'Problem is when you lot get interested in some-one, it sometimes means chokey and if that happens to one of my customers, and it's happened before, then I don't get paid.'

'What's this? A bill?'

'It's a bill all right and hand delivered. It's the third. I sent the first two by post but he's never paid, so I thought I'd make sure this time that there weren't any Post Office slip-ups.'

'Can I open it?'

'Sure.'

It was from Albert Soames, Litho Printers, 76 Fortune Way, Twickenham, Middlesex.

'Are you Albert Soames?' Leo asked.

'No, I'm Stephen. Albert was my father.'

Leo looked back at the bill. All it said was, 'To Account Rendered £1,750.'

'Can I ask what you did for Kendrick?'

'I'm a printer. I printed.'

'What?'

'Oh, boxes. Flat boxes. For pizzas. American I

211

think they were, called Wells Fargo something or
other.'

Leo had the kind of feeling archaeologists get
when they come upon shards of ancient pottery.

'Did you meet Kendrick?'

'Once. He came to give us the order.'

'You'd never seen him before?'

'Never.'

'Would you recognize him if you saw him again?'

'Yeah. I think so.'

'OK, let's go and have a coffee and we can talk.'

Macrae saw Marge Loftus standing by a grey Ford
Escort outside Clematis Court. He paid off the taxi
and went along the road towards her. She had been
a good-looking woman once. Now she was in her
fifties and had the worn appearance of someone who
knows about trouble.

Macrae knew her of old. The first time he had
met her was in the line of duty when he was still a
uniformed constable. He'd been called to a house in
Ealing after neighbours had reported hearing
screams. He'd found her on the staircase with a
broken jaw and bruised ribs. The husband who had
beaten her was drinking rum in the kitchen.

In those days the police tended to treat battered
wives as part of a 'domestic' in which they tried
not to get involved. But Macrae was new to such
philosophies and arrested the husband. He then pur-

sued the case, saw the husband taken to court and then heard him given a suspended sentence.

Macrae, who was on the beat in Ealing at the time, told Marge Loftus to call him if her situation didn't improve. It didn't. She called. Macrae arrested her husband again. He was given a second suspended sentence.

The next time he beat up his wife Macrae, who had not long before given up a promising boxing career, took him out into his garden and broke his nose. He then took Marge home with him to his new wife Linda and they looked after her for a couple of weeks. Soon afterwards the first refuge for battered wives was founded and Marge went there to work. She was now running her own refuge and from time to time took calls from George about battered women – and did something about them. This she always thought of as a repayment to fate for having had someone take an interest in her before she was beaten to death or permanently disfigured.

'I'm glad you could come, George,' she said.

'What happened?'

'She left during the night or early this morning. All I know is, she was gone at breakfast time. No one saw her leave and she'd defused the alarm.'

'So?'

'I phoned her flat.' She indicated the block ahead of them. 'Directory Inquiries gave me the number. She must have been home because either she or the little girl, Sally, lifted the phone. Then whoever it was put it down again. When I tried a few moments later it was engaged.'

'Either someone phoning in or they'd taken it off the hook.'

'A telephone makes a terrible noise these days if you leave it off the hook.'

'You put a pillow over it.'

'Anyway, I came here and rang the bell and knocked on the door but nothing happened. I *know* she's in there but she's not answering. And I thought, What if her husband comes home? So I phoned you.'

'Let's go and have a look.'

They walked to the small block of flats. They could see Mrs Lightly's balcony. There was no light on in the room behind it.

They went up the stairs to the open corridor. The dirty curtain still obscured what Macrae had thought was the kitchen window.

He rang the bell and waited but there was no movement. He bent down, pushed the letter flap and spoke into the oblong space. 'Mrs Lightly? It's George Macrae from Cannon Row. You remember, I was here before.'

Silence.

'We talked about your husband's promotion board, remember?'

There was a faint noise, he thought. It sounded like water running out of a bath.

'Mrs Lightly?'

Marge Loftus said, 'Let me.' She crouched down

beside Macrae and said, 'Cindy, it's me again, Marge Loftus. I asked George to come out with me because I'm frightened of what may happen to you and to Sally. I've known George a long time. He's a good friend and you can trust him. It was George who told me about you and said he thought I should look after you. That's how much he cares about you and Sally.'

She put her ear to the letter flap and whispered to George, 'Can you hear something?'

'I thought it was water,' he whispered back.

She shook her head and turned back to the flap. 'Cindy, if you won't think of yourself, think of Sally. We talked about her, remember? We said how great it was going to be for her to go to school and how great it was that you'd be at the refuge not worrying about yourself any longer . . . and how happy that would make her . . . and the friends she'd have . . . Don't you remember?'

Silence.

Marge stood up and flexed her aching knees. 'So what do we do now? We can't force her to come back with us.'

'Let me have another go.'

He bent down again.

'Mrs Lightly, we've done the best we can for you. What I'm going to do now is get in touch with the Social Services and tell them about your daughter. They will contact Sergeant Lightly and explain to him what's going on. Do you understand what I'm saying? I warn you, it will all get very heavy after that.'

He stuck his ear to the letter flap, but all he could hear was the faint sound of water.

He turned to Marge Loftus. 'You sure she's in there?'

'Not absolutely, but where else would she go?'

'Christ, my knees are giving in.' He came up slowly, his hand on the door. 'Oh damn!'

'What?'

'A splinter.' He sucked at his finger. Then he bent down again. 'Look at this.'

Where the door closed on the rebate there were a dozen nasty splinters and pieces of split wood.

'It wasn't like that before,' he said. 'There was a chain just about level with the splinters.'

He tried the door but it was locked.

'If Lightly came back last night he probably hammered the chain off and the wood got bruised.'

'And if he was still there when she came back?'

'Aye, I'd thought of that.' He pushed down the door handle. 'I'm not much good at this, but I'll have a go.' He jammed his right shoulder against the door. It was cheap, like the flat, and he felt it give.

'Don't stand too close,' he said. He took a step back and launched himself at the door. This time the lock burst and the door opened. There was a small corridor and the doors leading from it were closed which meant that the flat was in semi-darkness. They stood in silence for a moment. The sound of running water was louder.

'Cindy!' Marge Loftus called. 'Cindy! Sally!'

Macrae opened the door which led into the kitchen, and here the sound of water was strongest.

'Oh, my God!' Marge said.

DS Lightly was lying on his back on the floor. His hands were holding the handle of what looked to Macrae like an eight-inch kitchen knife. There was blood all over the place. His eyes were closed and he was not breathing. Above him was a kettle he might have been filling at the kitchen sink. The tap in the basin was running.

'Listen!' Marge said.

Macrae switched off the tap. They could hear someone crying softly. He opened the door opposite and saw a sight he would never forget: Mrs Lightly was lying on her bed with her arms around Sally.

They were both alive but both badly damaged. The woman's mouth had been bleeding. Sally's right eye was badly swollen and closed.

'Cindy?' Marge Loftus said. 'Oh God, Cindy, what's happened?'

And then Mrs Lightly spoke. At first her mouth would not work properly, then the words came out and Macrae realized she had lost teeth.

'He hit Sally,' she said. 'I couldn't have that.'

Chapter Twenty

'My father hated photo litho and what he called the new-fangled forms of printing,' Stephen Soames said. 'He was really a hot-metal man; worked originally for the old *Daily Herald* as a linotype operator.'

Leo's mind was not on printing. They were sitting in his dented Golf in Castlenau with a view of the house Goater's 'boys' said belonged to a Michael Knight, and which he now knew also belonged to a Roland Christie and a Chris Roland and a Martin Kendrick – that's if Stephen Soames was able to give a positive ID.

'Do you live in places like this if you're a printer?' Leo indicated the beautiful houses lining Castlenau. 'You sure as hell don't if you're a policeman.'

'We should be making pizzas. Like Mr Knight.'

Leo knew he was fishing but did not rise. He had not mentioned drugs, just that Knight was suspected of 'committing a felony'.

'How long's he likely to be?' Soames looked at his watch. 'I told my staff I'd be away for an hour or so.' Leo did not reply.

'What if he goes out the back? What if he doesn't come out?' Soames said.

'He will. The woman in the secretarial office said he came there every day and she was positive he hadn't been.'

'Even so . . .'

'Look, this is a chance we had to take. If he doesn't show in an hour I take you back to your car and we postpone the ID until tomorrow. We'll have the whole place under surveillance. He won't be going anywhere. All you've got to do is your part.'

'It'd be easier if the woman was with him.'

'What woman?'

'The one that came when he ordered the boxes.'

'You didn't mention a woman. What did she look like?'

'Tall. Very thin. Good looking.'

'How old?'

'Thirtyish?'

'Did you get a name?'

Soames shook his head. 'I remember her as being bloody nervous.'

'Why?'

'No reason that I could see. You know who she is?'

'Maybe,' Leo said.

They sat for another hour but no one left the house. Leo took Soames back to his car in Paddington then drove back to Cannon Row.

The place was in uproar. He saw Wilson and Scales hurrying along the corridor and asked the station officer what was going on.

'You haven't heard?'

'Heard *what*?'

'About Lightly?'

'*What* about Lightly?'

'He was murdered this morning.'

'Jesus! By anyone we know?'

The desk sergeant looked to see they were alone then said, 'They're bringing in his wife.'

'What happened?'

The sergeant opened his mouth then closed it. Macrae came in the door followed by a woman and a child, a policewoman and another woman.

Macrae saw Leo and said, 'Something's come up, laddie. Wait for me here.'

'Right, guv'nor.'

The party went into Wilson's office and the desk sergeant filled him in as best he could about the killing. 'Scales is spitting blood,' he said softly and Leo could understand why. Scales did not like bad situations – or what he liked to call 'negative things' – happening in case they rubbed off on him.

For most of the remainder of the day Leo did what he liked least: he waited for Macrae. He wrote a report on what had occurred that morning and he organized a surveillance of Knight's house. Then he went on waiting.

But Macrae had forgotten all about him and all

about the case they had been working on. Wilson's room had filled up with people. There was a woman now from the Social Services as well as someone wanting to know what to tell the media.

Macrae disregarded them and concentrated on Lucinda Lightly. She was sitting in one of Wilson's office chairs and her daughter was standing between her knees. Macrae was on one side of her and Mrs Loftus on the other.

Wilson said, 'Mrs Lightly, do you know what is going to happen to you?'

'They're going to put me in gaol.' Her mouth was in such a state it sounded as though she was talking Portuguese.

Macrae cut in: 'No they're not. What's going to happen is this: you'll be taken to court tomorrow and you'll be remanded on bail and—'

'Macrae!'

Scales was standing at the door.

'I want to see you. And you too, Les.'

They went to Scales's room. They weren't asked to sit down.

'What was all that supposed to mean?' Scales said to Macrae, flicking his ballpoint pen angrily.

'What was all what supposed to mean?' Macrae was smoking a cigar and did not consider putting it out.

'How the hell do you know she'll be remanded? It's got nothing to do with you!'

'Of course it has.'

'Hang on a sec—' Wilson began, but neither Scales nor Macrae acknowledged his presence.

Scales said, 'Perhaps you haven't fully taken in what's happened. One of my men has been murdered and you . . .'

'Murdered?'

'Of course.'

'Whatever happened to the concept of self-defence?'

'You have to prove self-defence.'

'You have to prove murder.'

Scales paused. Flick . . . flick . . . went the pen. In a softer voice he said, 'Listen, George, what we know is this: Lightly was found in the kitchen with a knife in his stomach. His wife and daughter were in the bedroom where his wife complained of him hitting the child. Did you ever hit one of your children?'

'Of course.'

'Les?'

'Well . . .'

'And did your wives try to murder you? Course not. Stands to reason.'

Macrae said, 'He's been abusing her for months. Maybe years.'

'Maybe,' Scales said. 'Today he hit his daughter. At least that's what his wife says. But for all we know she might have hit her daughter herself.'

'I don't believe this!' Macrae said. 'I spoke to her earlier. I know what was happening.'

'You don't know anything of the sort. Or at least what you should know with your experience in the force is that nothing – and I mean nothing – is as it seems at first.'

'Are you saying that she made all this up?'

'I'm saying she could have. And I'm saying it's not up to you to make judgements. She goes to court. The magistrate makes the decision.'

Macrae said, 'You know as well as I do that she'll be remanded in custody and that Sally will be taken into care.'

'That's how it works. You kill someone, you get arrested, you go to court and you get remanded in custody.'

Macrae said, 'I want her to go back with Madge Loftus to the refuge. That's where she should have been all along.'

Les said, 'She can't, George. And you know she can't.'

Macrae dropped his cigar on the floor and stamped on it. 'This is about image,' he said. 'You're going to try to whitewash that bastard Lightly and—'

'I'm not going to do anything of the kind!' Scales said.

'—and Les is going to help you. Mustn't smear the good name of Cannon Row. Well, to hell with that. If I get my say in court I'm going to tell what I know.'

'George . . .' Click . . . click . . . 'Listen to me—'

Macrae broke across him, 'Les, you remember the Dibby case? It was something like this. They removed the child into care and how long was it before the mother got her back?'

'About a year, I think.'

'And the mother was innocent!'

Wilson said, 'There may have been other factors. I can't remember now.'

Macrae said, 'Why not just let her go to the refuge for tonight and then she can go to court tomorrow morning and Marge can get her a decent lawyer and perhaps he can get the charge reduced. If she goes in now it'll be for murder.'

'And that's what it *was*,' Scales said.

'You weren't there. You never saw Mrs Lightly. The rota doctor examined her. He said some of her facial wounds and the broken teeth were fresh.'

Les said, 'It's not for you to decide, George. It's not the way the system works.'

'Anyway, how the hell were you involved in this?' Scales said.

'I had a tip-off from an informer.'

They waited for him to continue but he remained silent. Scales shrugged. 'Right,' he said. 'That's all.'

Ten minutes later Mrs Lightly was charged and taken off to the cells. A woman from the Social Services took Sally away. Macrae stayed in his office, aware of what was happening and aware that his rage had brought on the worst attack of fibrillation he had ever experienced. He sat down at his desk and put his head on his blotter.

That was how Leo found him. 'You all right, guv'nor?'

'Aye. I'm fine. Away you go home.'

Chapter Twenty-One

Leo parked the Golf in Putney and walked towards Laura's house. He was excited, apprehensive, wound up like a violin string on the point of snapping. He had been getting to this point since that morning when Martin Kendrick had entered his life – if only as a name.

Since then his mind had been racing and stopping, racing and stopping. He had needed Macrae, but Macrae had been unavailable. He had needed someone. No, not someone, just Macrae.

But how the hell could he explain, even to Macrae, that he'd been screwing someone who was asking him to trace a man who might have committed a murder? That she was the sister of a woman who had been railroaded to gaol on trumped-up drug-smuggling charges and who, if Leo was guessing correctly, might also get the chop if she found the man? If he'd killed one person, why not two?

Macrae was Macrae. He could become involved in situations like that and if necessary talk about them. Leo couldn't – except possibly to Macrae.

So what was he doing?

He was following a lead by himself because his boss was involved in something he believed was more important than a druggy murder.

Eventually no one – except her father – would give a bugger if Julia Maddox was buried and forgotten and her murderer forgotten too. But you didn't kill a cop without all hell breaking loose – even if you were his wife. And from what Leo had gathered Cannon Street, or at least Scales, was looking for a way to sanitize and homogenize and generally put the Lightly killing into a different category, i.e., that Lightly was a good copper who got done by a bad wife.

But if what he had heard about Macrae's attitude was true, that wasn't going to work, and as the argument raged he, Leo was on his own.

He rang Laura's bell and when she opened the door all he could think about was how attractive she looked.

'Hi,' she said. 'I wondered if it was you.'

'Oh?'

'Come in. You got my message?'

'No.'

'You just came? Better and better.'

She was in a pair of white track suit bottoms, a white rolltop sweater and a headband. As usual her feet were bare. They sat on the cushions facing each other. It was curious, he thought, her feet did not look like women's feet. The nails were very short and they looked square and hard – but attractive.

'I left a message asking you to ring,' she said.

'I didn't get it. We've had a hell of a day.' He told her briefly about Lightly. 'My guv'nor brought his wife in. She'd been battered and so had her daughter.'

She looked over his shoulder as though at something beyond him and then said, 'Is the wife a nice woman?'

'No idea. Why?'

'It's the kind of thing that happens to nice women. Let's have a drink.'

'Listen, I can't stay,' he said. 'I'm on a job. I've just brought this back.' He held up the Journal.

She got to her feet. 'White wine OK?'

He heard her open the fridge in the kitchen. The sitting-room was as he recalled it. There were the same musical instruments and prayer wheels but something had been added. It was the head of a store mannequin with frizzy black hair. It looked at him blankly from a table by the wall.

She came back with two glasses of wine and gave him one.

'Cheers.'

'Slainté, as my guv'nor would say.'

She smiled at him as he drank. It was the smile he had first seen in the hospital ward, a wonderfully involving smile.

He said, 'Have you taken your car in yet?'

'Not yet. But definitely tomorrow.'

'And you'll let me know.'

'Of course. So you finished the Journal?'

He nodded.

'That's why I called you,' she said. 'I hoped you had. I wanted your reaction before I called Sam again. What did you think of it? I mean I gave it to you for a purpose.'

'I found it fascinating. And I can quite see why you want to help Samantha so much. It's a terrible injustice. That's if it's completely factual.'

'Why shouldn't it be?'

'Prison may have distorted her view of herself and what happened.'

'I know Sam. It's the naked truth.'

'OK. But there were a couple of things I wondered about.'

'Shoot.'

'You told me Sam had been married to Kendrick. But it doesn't say anything about that in the Journal.'

'Did I say married? I don't think so.'

'I thought you did.'

'I must have meant it in an emotional sense.'

'But she only knew him a few days.'

'You don't have to know someone for years to feel that kind of emotion. Look what he did to her. For God's sake don't you think he owes her something?'

'Of course.'

'I mean, you believe the Journal, don't you?'

'If you say it's factual then I do. Is she thinking of trying to get it published?'

'Of course not. Why?'

'These Thai cases are in the news when they happen but then . . . I always want to know what becomes of the people involved.'

She watched him over the lip of her glass and said, 'What was the other thing?'

'The other thing?'

'You said you wondered about a couple of things in the Journal.'

'Oh yes. Well, this isn't directly from the Journal. It's just that I wondered if she was doing anything to help herself.'

'How do you mean?'

'There are organizations that help ex-prisoners. Has she been to see any of them?'

'That's not the sort of thing Sam would do.'

'Why not?'

'She's too naked, too insecure.' She sipped her drink. 'It goes back a long time to when she was a kid. Her father was killed in a car accident and after that her mother used to bring a lot of "uncles" home. You know what I mean?'

'I think so.'

'Do you know, I can remember my mother reading to me in bed only once! And that's what I wanted more than anything. Her sitting with me at night before I went to sleep.'

He was startled at the depth of passion she had put into the words.

'You know all these "home-alone" kids we hear

about now? I can tell you there's nothing new in it. She used to go out a lot. Stay out. You know what that does to you?'

'What?'

'It makes you insecure.'

'And that's what happened to Samantha?' he said. 'She was made insecure?'

'Right. Very insecure. Especially with men. All the "uncles", you know. The problem was love. She didn't seem to get any love. That's important for a child.'

'Vital.'

'Yes, vital. Not that there was much love of any kind in the house. It wasn't love that operated there.'

'Did you feel the same insecurity?'

'Me insecure? You think so?'

'I didn't say you were.'

'You contradict me, Leo. That's not very nice. And there's something else that's not very nice: you came here and we made love but since then you haven't even picked up the phone.'

He was thrown by her sudden changes of mood. 'I'm sorry. But you were so anxious about the Journal I wanted to finish it before phoning and coming to see you again.'

'Well, now you've come. What plans have you got?'

'Sorry?'

'I like to know.'

'You mean—?'

'Of course. Is that what you want? Sex?'

Her face had hardened and so had her eyes. Her voice had become crisp.

A wild thought entered his brain.

It was so wild that it almost spilled out but he managed to check it and said softly, 'Do you?'

'You know, Leo, I have a feeling about you. You said you weren't married but I have this feeling—'

'I'm not. And you can believe it or not as you like.'

It was as though he had slapped her face. She flinched and her eyes lit up with anger. She was a different person. And once he had convinced himself of that there was no stopping the progression of his thoughts.

'Is sex what Samantha wants?' he said.

'Samantha? What's she got to do with it?'

'I thought she had everything to do with it. I thought that's who I was talking to.'

She smiled but there was no warmth now. 'Talking to Samantha? You've never even met her.'

'I'm beginning to think I have. You're Samantha, aren't you? I know you're Laura, but you're also the sister you made up because you couldn't tell a cop who you were. Isn't that the case?'

She rose and poured herself more wine. She looked down at him for a long moment before saying, 'What would you have done?'

'I don't know and that's the honest truth.'

'You're not a very good detective. I wasn't really trying to hide it. I think I wanted you to find out.'

'That's not true, you were trying to hide it.'

Again her face hardened. 'That's the second time,' she said.

'Second time what?'

'That you've called me a liar. When did you come to the conclusion that there was no Samantha?'

'It must have been in the back of my mind. I never met her so I wasn't able to inject life into her, not from your description. And then, a little while ago, you used the word "naked" in the same sense that the Journal uses it.'

'That's good, Leo.'

'But I really think it came when you were telling me about the background with your mother. I could see that and I could see it happening to you. You were passionate about it and it was *you* not Samantha. That's the feeling I got and if I'm wrong I'm sorry because if I'm not it changes things and the truth becomes harder and harder to find.'

Suddenly she leaned towards him and said, 'You want to know the truth? The real truth? You think you can handle it? You want to know why they fucked me up in Bangkok? Yes *me* . . . *me* . . . You were right about that. Well, I'll tell you, Leo. Martin and Jane had been up to their skulls in the drug traffic. They were going to be put away for ever. And Martin might have been hanged. So they made a deal with the Thais. They'd trap foreigners for the Thai Drugs Squad. I wasn't the only one. In the space of four months they trapped two Germans, an

American boy, a French girl and a Swede.'

She lit a cigarette. It was the first time he had seen her smoke apart from the marijuana.

'Martin came to see me in Bangkok gaol. He brought the Captain. He probably had half a dozen bears and you know why? Because he was becoming like a ventriloquist. He couldn't speak to anyone else. I saw a ventriloquist interviewed once without his dummy and each time he answered a question he looked down to his arm where the dummy should have been. That's how Martin was with the bear.

'He told me he was sorry but that the Captain said Martin's life was more important than my life. He was quite honest. And the whole bit in the airport with Jane was just another set-up in case I found the drugs and got rid of them. He knew I trusted Jane completely.'

Her face seemed to have lost some of its attractiveness and to have become gaunt and bony.

She said, 'You think you can imagine what six years are like in a Thai gaol?'

'No, I can't.'

'Well, that's honest too. I would have died there without Barbie. She taught me to defend myself both physically and mentally. She taught me The Way.'

'Was she your lover?' Leo said.

It was another question that had risen in his mind and this time it had spilled out into speech.

'That's brave of you, Leo. Men don't like talking to women about lesbianism.'

'It would explain some things.'

'That's what you like, isn't it? Being a detective, you like explanations. OK, I'll explain. Yes, she was my lover. She was also my saviour.'

'Did she know you were also Sam?'

'For Christ's sake, I thought you were brighter than this! She *invented* Sam. She wanted me to have both a feminine name and a masculine name.'

'Is that The Way?'

'No, Leo. Maybe some day I'll tell you about The Way.'

'And I'll tell you about Snakes and Ladders, because I think that's what we've both been playing.'

'Snakes and ladders?'

'The board game. You've played it?'

'Of course.'

'I think you played it with Martin Kendrick without knowing it. You thought you were going up the ladders, but *he* was going up the ladders, and you were going down the snakes. And something similar was happening to me. My guv'nor and I are investigating a nasty murder and he was going up the ladders in what he was finding out, and I was going down the snakes in what I *wasn't* finding out, so that when I did come across something we were a long way apart.'

'You're losing me.'

'We knew who Martin Kendrick was and at the same time we *didn't* know. This is thinking aloud. Some of it's wild but I'll try to explain. You see, his real name isn't Kendrick and he lives not too far from where we are now. We've been finding out about him but I never knew he was your Martin Kendrick. But that's life and it's also police work. My guv'nor believes most cases are solvable if you can get to what people know. The trouble is that sometimes they don't know they know. And it was happening to us: we knew but didn't know.'

'Knew what, Leo?'

'Pieces began to come together this morning And others have joined up since I arrived here. Now you're going to say you meant me to know.'

'Know what?'

This was what everything had been leading to. Some of it he had led; some had led him. He felt apprehensive. If he went on he was deep into all sorts of shit. If he didn't . . .

'About Jane, or Julia, as she's really called.'

'You want another drink, Leo?'

'Just half a glass.'

'Mustn't drink on duty, isn't that the phrase?'

'Something like that.'

She gave him the wine.

'Julia?' she said.

'That nasty murder I mentioned . . . the girl's name was Julia, but I think she was your Jane, the Jane from Bangkok.'

'You *think*? Is this the modern detective? Someone who thinks?'

'Absolutely, dear.'

'Don't call me dear. I'm not your dear, OK?'

'OK. Right. But let me go back to something Macrae said. He asked me if women wore wigs and I said only old women as far as I knew. But I didn't know much, did I? Store window mannequins wear wigs but not as well made as that one.' He pointed to the head on the table. 'That's a real wig.'

'So you're an expert on wigs.'

'I don't know a thing about wigs, but we found out about them. There were hairs in Julia's bed. Some came from the men she'd been sleeping with and some came from a wig. I think if we took samples of the hair from your wig and analysed them we'd find they were the same: Asian hair dyed.'

'Why Asian hair dyed, Leo?'

'Because it's relatively cheap. That's what we found out. And someone who was going to deal with Julia/Jane and wanted to wear a wig so she could not be identified wouldn't necessarily buy an expensive one, would she?'

'And what did this person do when she went into the apartment in her wig, Leo?'

'I don't know, but I can guess. She went in to get information. Julia/Jane was tortured and I assume it was for a reason. That's what it was all about, wasn't it? Say this person, this woman, had been unjustly imprisoned in Thailand, wouldn't she want some recompense when she came out of gaol? I think I'd want a decent sum for those years. But first she'd have to find the people who'd put her away.

How? What about prison? Lots of druggies in Puckle-hurst, and all with those little pieces of information my guv'nor likes to talk about? Or newspaper files? Drug cases. Pictures. Or—'

'Not very clever, Leo. What you're talking about now is coincidence, long shots, like saying the Woman in Question walked down the King's Road one day and there in front of her was the Other Woman in Question. It doesn't work like that. No, the Woman in Question already knew the Other Woman's real name before she left Bangkok. One of the other foreigners had seen her passport and so she knew she was Julia not Jane. And Maddox isn't a rare name. Not common, but not rare either. So you get the London phone book and start there and you dial the Maddoxes and you ask for Julia. You say you don't want to speak to her, just check her address.'

'And if she'd been married and changed her name?'

'You'd go to the Public Record office where marriages are registered. You learn things in prison, Leo. You also learn about justice and injustice. You should know about that, in the police. That's all I want. Justice.'

'I'm only in the justice business as a servant,' he said.

'I want you to help me, Leo.'

'That's how this whole thing started, isn't it? You've just mentioned coincidence. This whole thing, you and me sitting here talking about what happened, sounds like coincidence but it isn't. Because I've remembered, which I wasn't supposed to remember, that when we were taking you to hospital the police radio went off in the car. You knew right then that I was a cop and you used me just like you were used in Bangkok. It was you who dragged me into this.'

As he spoke he began to feel a new sensation of anger.

'Why would I do that?'

'To help you find Martin Kendrick, of course. Who better than a cop?'

She ignored his answer and said, 'That doesn't answer my point about justice.'

'Let me tell you that my guv'nor's going down the same road as you over a murdered copper's wife and he probably won't win justice for her either. What else did you learn in prison? How to kill?'

'You really want to know? OK I'll be honest. I learned everything there is to learn . . .' You said you'd want . . . what was the word, recompense? I'll stay with that word. But what you meant was money. I don't care about money. I've got enough. My mother died and, surprise, surprise, there was enough to keep me. So the recompense I want is something different.'

'I can understand that.'

She stared at him for a moment and then said, 'You know, Leo, you probably think you're an intelli-

gent guy, but you're not really. You couldn't understand anything. I wonder how long you'd last in a
Thai prison.'

'I'd last.'

'Would you? I don't think you'd even last in a
Thai women's prison.'

'Because I don't know The Way?'

'That and other things. Let's take the present
case. You think I murdered Julia, don't you?'

'Yes, I do.'

'Maybe you're right. And maybe you're right
about going to her flat to get information. But how
the hell can you prove it?'

'I can't. And that's the truth.'

'You've got nothing. What you really want is a
written confession. That's how the police like it –
and not only in this country. I've been through it,
don't forget. Or at least Sam has. They make you
write down everything and then they get you to sign
it. And—'

'Oh, Jesus!' Leo said. 'You wanted an address and
a name. Of course! The yellow paper! Listen, you . . .
well, maybe not you . . . Sam tortured her. Sam
stuffed paper in her mouth and asked her where
Kendrick was and she was beginning to write it
down . . .'

'Are you guessing here?'

'Not at all. We found the yellow Post-it slip. But
all we could get were impressions. You . . . Sam . . .
threw it in the loo. Remember?'

'Yes, I remember.'

She stood up and poured herself more wine. She held the bottle out but he refused. He too rose and began to pace up and down the space between the cushions.

He said, '*M* . . . *I* . . . that's what she wrote. I thought it was the beginning of a word like Mi . . . lk . . . something written for the milkman perhaps. But what about Mi . . . ke . . . That's what she was writing. Mike. And she was going to tell you the truth. Because that's his real name. Michael . . . And then she died, choking for breath.'

'That's awfully good, Leo,' she said.

And then she hit him.

He was still caught up in his rushing thought process and was totally unprepared.

The blow was violent and accurate. It caught him on the side of the neck. His body tumbled down on to the cushions and the side of his head and neck and shoulder seemed to become paralysed.

'You're very naïve, Leo,' she said. 'You came in to see Laura but you found Sam instead. I suppose you didn't really have it all sorted out but when you knew you were getting close you should have been more careful.' She sipped a little wine. 'That blow was a lamington, by the way. Being a highly trained and intelligent policeman you'll know it by its real karate name, *choku-zuki*, which translated means straight punch. But Barbie and I called it a lamington.'

Leo turned on his side and began to raise himself on his hands and knees.

'And this is bangers and mash,' she said, and kicked him in the face.

Blood poured down into his mouth from his nose and he knew he had also bitten his tongue. He tried to say something but it was as though he was talking with a mouthful of water.

She said, 'Of course you won't know it as bangers and mash, you'll realize it is *yoko-geri-keage*, the side snap kick, which is used at close range to vulnerable areas of the body. You see, Leo, in the gaol Barbie and I had to use a secret language so that we could protect ourselves. Not much point in knowing martial arts when everybody else knows how you're going to react to an attack. Surprise is everything. So if we were under threat and she said, "steak-and-eggs" I would do this,' and she caught Leo by the hair and smashed his head against the wall. As he fell forward she brought her knee up into his face.

'That was steak and eggs,' she said. 'Of course that doesn't come from any of the martial arts you'd read about in books. That was one we made up but I think you'll agree it works well. Prison walls are hard, you know.'

She gave herself a little more wine, then said, '*Don't bite me!*'

She laughed contemptuously, 'Do you remember saying that? It was enough to make me puke, Leo.

Don't bite me. Don't flatter yourself! You're no lover. It takes a woman to serve a woman.'

Slowly Leo was pushing himself up the wall. She waited until he had regained his feet then she grabbed his wrist and brought him crashing down on to his head. 'That was *yonkajo*, as I'm sure you know. And of course we've now entered aikido . . . Harmony . . . Energy . . . The Way.'

Leo was snorting blood.

She said, 'You asked me about The Way, do you remember? I could use words like reflection, understanding, enlightenment, but you wouldn't understand. You're a policeman so you follow a different Way. And this is your Way: you will be hurt and humiliated and brought to heel.'

Again he travelled up the wall. His body felt numb and heavy. Slowly, like some strange serpent, his arm and fist rose in the air. It was in his mind that he must use it against her, somehow he must hit her. She took his outstretched arm and brought him somersaulting past her on to the floor.

'*Kote gaeshi dori*,' she said. He lay crumpled up. His shirt was covered in blood.

'We called that pavlova,' she said. 'You start off crisp like meringue but if I do that to you several times, you become soft, like the top of a pavlova.'

She crouched down in front of him. 'Lamingtons are little cakes and pavlovas are desserts and both come from Australia. That's why Barbie called them that.'

She rose, leaned against a table and watched him. He had never really recovered from her very first unexpected blow. That side of his head and neck were still semi-paralysed.

She said, 'Now I want you to listen carefully. You know why I was at Julia's and you know why I used the sandwich-maker. And I can do that to you. I don't have to stuff paper into your mouth because you're in my place and there's no one in the flat upstairs so it doesn't matter if you scream. You know what I want Leo. I want Martin Kendrick's address and his name. OK?'

Leo tried to speak again but all that emerged was a sound of pain and suffering.

' "Don't bite me," you said. Well, I won't bite you but I'm going to hurt you if you don't give me that name and address.'

She caught him by the hair. He lunged at her. She kicked him across his face and this time he knew she had broken his nose.

'That's only for starters,' she said.

He lay on his face on the hard floor and she took one of his arms and twisted it behind him. 'Leo, I'm going to break it if you don't tell me where he is!'

He knew, in the red cave in which he seemed to exist, that she was telling the truth.

'Tell me!'

He moaned. He tried to talk but his broken lips and swollen tongue made the words incomprehensible.

She dropped his arm and threw him the kitchen towel she'd used on the wine bottle. He brought up the blood in his mouth and throat.

'Tell me, Leo.'

He spoke slowly and with great difficulty but he told her.

She said, 'I'm glad you didn't try to play the hero, like telling me to fuck off as they do in the movies.'

He tried to speak again but blood came out of his mouth.

'Bangers and mash,' she said, and kicked him again. This time he collapsed completely.

Chapter Twenty-Two

'So you're trying to rape me and I'm not going to let you,' Frenchy said. 'I'm going to break your arm.'

'That's a wee bit unfriendly,' Macrae said. 'What about The Way? Why don't you do that and not break my arm.'

'That's aikido, this is judo. And it's about being attacked, OK?'

They were in his house in Battersea. Frenchy had finally had enough of planchette and had phoned him to collect her. It had been precisely what he needed after the row with Scales and the guilt he had felt about the Lightly case. Now, a bottle and a half of Australian sparkling Chardonnay later, they were both naked on Macrae's big double bed.

'You know what I suggest?' he said. 'I suggest we get on with what we came to bed for.'

'I just wanted to show you—'

The phone rang. He leaned over and picked up the receiver. 'Macrae . . .' he said.

There was a long silence.

'George Macrae . . .' he said.

Again there was silence.

'Oh, Christ.' He was about to put down the phone when he heard a faint voice.

'Guv'nor . . .'

'Silver. Is that you?'

'Guv'nor . . .'

'Are you hurt? Take it slowly now. Tell me where you are.'

There was a retching sound and then Silver's voice became clearer and he gave Macrae the address.

'Don't move. Stay where you are.'

Macrae hurriedly began to dress. 'It's Silver,' he said to Frenchy. 'Something bad's happened.'

It took him, driving through red lights, less than twenty minutes to reach the house in Putney. He found Silver in the ethnic room. He had managed to pull himself to his feet and was leaning against the wall.

Macrae saw his face. 'Oh, Christ, laddie, what have they done to you?'

'I'm all right, guv'nor,' Leo whispered.

'Don't talk bullshit. I'm going to get an ambulance.'

'I'm better than I was when I phoned. Please don't call an ambulance.'

'Let's see what you look like with the blood gone. Where's the bathroom? We'll get you cleaned up and you can talk at the same time.'

Slowly Silver recovered. The cold water on his

face stung. His nose was broken and he was in pain in a hundred different places but he knew now that he was not going to die.

He talked as he was washed.

'A woman?' Macrae was appalled. 'A woman did this?'

'She's no ordinary woman.' In a voice filled with shame, Leo said, 'So I told her what she wanted to know. I'm sorry as hell.'

'Don't be silly, laddie. You've taken a hell of a lot of punishment. You did the only thing you could. I'll get you to hospital.'

'Guv'nor, please ... Let's just get to Knight's house ...'

'Don't be a bloody fool.'

'I want to see her taken.'

Macrae paused. Then he said, 'I bet you do. Come on then.'

Two detectives, organized earlier by Silver, were watching the house from a van on the opposite side of the street. One of them, DC Lansing, said, 'A woman went in about an hour ago. No one's come out.'

Macrae said, 'The woman's dangerous. So's Knight. We need more troops, so get on the radio and—'

At that moment, in the clear cold air, there was the unmistakable sound of a gunshot in the house.

'Jesus,' Macrae said. 'Does he have a family?'

'There's another woman and two small kids,' Lansing said.

'We can't wait then. You two take the rear but radio for back-up. Don't suppose you drew side-arms?'

'No, sir.'

'Don't do anything rash. We're not looking for medals. And wait till you hear me call.'

He watched the two detectives move into the drive and then round the back of the house.

'This isn't what I like doing,' he said to Silver. 'But a woman with kids . . . You stay in the car and—'

'Guv'nor, I'm coming.'

There was something about the tone that reminded Macrae of Frenchy. He shrugged. 'The sympathy's gone out of the window, laddie. On your own broken head be it.'

They kept to the lawns and shrubberies and reached the front of the house. As they did so they heard a child's scream come from one of the upstairs rooms.

'There's an open window,' Silver whispered.

It was a low sash window that gave into the dining-room, which was in darkness. Macrae pushed it up and climbed over the sill. Silver followed. They walked through the room and halted in the passageway.

They heard someone sobbing in one of the rooms upstairs.

'I'm going up,' Macrae said. 'You wait here. And that's a bloody order!'

He tiptoed to the base of the stairs and began to climb.

Leo stood in the dark passage. Ahead of him was a door, almost closed, under which a faint light showed. He pushed it and saw that it led into the drawing-room. He opened it a little more. On the floor he saw the booted foot of a man. He was lying between the fireplace and a big blue and gold brocaded sofa. He was wearing jeans, boots and a silk shirt drenched in blood. In the middle of the shirt was a hole more than an inch in diameter.

He went into the room and knelt by the body. He assumed it was Michael Knight. He put his head down by the face but could hear and feel no breathing.

He was about to straighten up when a woman's voice said, 'What took you so long? Even I could spot the van.'

The lights went on.

'Leo!' Laura said. 'I was expecting a copper all right, but you're a surprise. I don't mean that you're alive. I had no intention of killing you. I'm just surprised you got here.'

She moved away from the wall and sat in an occasional chair. She was wearing the same clothes as she had been though now her feet were encased in trainers. In her hand was a heavy pistol.

'Martin's,' she said, holding it up. 'I hope you don't mind if I call him Martin. He was Martin to me.'

Leo should have been afraid but wasn't. He had been humiliated, badly beaten, rendered almost useless as an officer of the law, not only out-fought, but out-thought. He was angry.

'Give me the gun, Laura,' he said. 'It's over.'

'It's not over until the fat lady sings, Leo, and I'm the fat lady tonight. I really didn't think you'd be the one who'd come. I thought you'd phone for help and then your pals would steam out here to pick me and Martin up.'

Leo took a pace towards her. He was listening all the while for Macrae. 'Give me the gun.'

'Oh no, Leo. Not the gun. The gun stays with me. I had to take it away from Martin. He was very concerned about his family – as if I would have touched his wife and kids. I tried to make him understand what was going to happen. I used your word. I said, "Martin, I am looking for recompense." And I'll tell you something interesting. At first he tried to pretend he didn't know me. This is someone who slept with me. Who held me in his arms and said he loved me. "You've got the wrong person," he said. "I am not Martin Kendrick." '

' "Oh, yes you are," I said . . . No, Leo! No closer. Just stand there by the sofa . . . "Yes, Martin, you are," I said. "You may be Mr Knight to the London police, but to the Thai prison authorities and to a series of people inside Bangkok prison you're Martin Kendrick." And he went on saying no, no he wasn't. And then you know what, Leo? Look under his body.'

Leo moved slowly backwards. He saw something wedged under Knight's body. What was visible was the orange arm of a teddy bear.

'I made it in Pucklehurst,' she said. 'Even to the

bandage round its head. And I brought it here tonight and I said, "I've brought you a present, Martin," and I gave it to him.'

'Laura, you've done enough damage,' Leo said. 'There are a dozen policemen round the house. It really is over.'

'Oh, I know that. It's what I said to Martin. I gave him the Captain and I said, "It's over, Martin," and he began to cry . . .'

Leo found his sympathies were with the man who knew his life was over.

Laura said, 'I did a lot of crying too, you know, Leo. You may find that hard to believe, but I did. I was still in Pucklehurst when they brought me Barbie's last letter. She was in bad trouble: money trouble, health trouble, police trouble. And she wrote and said she was packing it in. That was her phrase. Packing it in. And she did. She packed it in in a gas-filled car. And that's why I don't care any longer, Leo. I wanted my recompense and I got my recompense and in a second—'

'Laura, don't talk any more, don't—'

'—I'll also pack it in.'

And she put the heavy pistol into her mouth and blew the top of her head off.

Chapter Twenty-Three

A sunny Saturday morning and all was well with George Macrae.

He lay in his bed, sexually at peace, and listened to the noises in the kitchen which would eventually translate into a steaming cup of real coffee. He liked real coffee. When he was by himself he made instant but Frenchy had read in one of her magazines that if you didn't make coffee in a cafetière you were an unsophisticated berk – those had not been the precise words but it is what they had meant – so she had bought one and George was reaping the benefit.

Peace of any sort was unfamiliar territory to Macrae and, as he lay in bed, waiting for her return, he kept wondering if there was something just round the corner which he had not thought of yet and which was about to pounce on him.

He went over in his mind the recent events: the murder of Julia Maddox was solved. More importantly, the state of play in the Lightly case had gone his way. The Crown Prosecution Service, much to the chagrin of Scales, had charged Mrs Lightly with manslaughter, not murder, and she was out on bail and reunited with her child. She still had a case to fight but he knew she had an excellent chance of winning, especially with his evidence.

Then there was the return of Frenchy. That was the best happening so far. And the fact that his daughter Susan was on her slow way back to England. It would be good to see her again and to have the threat of sudden monetary catastrophe removed. And, not least, Silver was not badly hurt.

He put his hands over his ears and tried to listen to the inside of his head. He could hear nothing.

He took his pulse.

Bong . . . bong . . . bong . . . bong . . .

No sickening lurches. Everything normal.

That's what the consultant at the hospital had told him yesterday.

Macrae had sat in the waiting-room a long while and had spent about a minute and a half in the consultant's office. He was a thin middle-aged man with an expensive suit under his white coat. He had glanced briefly at Macrae's notes, then said, 'Nothing wrong with your heart at all. It's probably wind. Are you a heavy eater?'

'I like my food.'

'Do you drink?'

'In moderation.'

'Smoke?'

'Yes.'

'Then I don't know why you bother to come here. I mean, what can you expect? Tell me something: are you tense? do you get angry much?'

It was like handing Macrae a weapon. He rose and bent over the doctor as though he was about to lift him out of his chair and throw him through the hospital window. Then he said in a soft voice, 'Angry? Only when I have to wait an hour and a half for a National Health employee.'

The man had shrunk nervously into himself, which had given Macrae more pleasure than he had had for some time.

Now he heard Frenchy clinking the coffee mugs and he lifted himself so he lay against the head of the bed. The day loomed pleasantly empty. Lunch out? A curry? The afternoon in bed with Frenchy?

Sometime they'd have to talk about money.

But not today.

She came in carrying the mugs and the morning paper. She was wearing one of his shirts as usual and all sorts of goodies were bouncing and jigging underneath.

'Look at this, George.' She held up the paper and pointed to a photograph. 'This is the woman in the Maddox case. They've got her name wrong. They're calling her Laura. Her name's Sam.'

'How the hell do you know?'

'She was my teacher in the martial arts programme.'

Macrae sat up straighter. 'In your church hall?'

'Yeah. She was terrific. I mean I can't think of any bloke who could have stood up against her.'

Macrae thought of Silver.

He said, 'Is that what you want? To come back here and beat the bejabers out of me?'

'Nah. I think I'll give it up. I never really enjoyed it.'

'What about The Way?'

'Never understood that. They talked about it enough but didn't really explain it. If the worst comes to the worst I'll probably just lie back and think of Britain.'

Macrae decided not to correct her. It was too nice a day for that. And if this was The Way, he was all for it.

A sunny Saturday morning and all was not well with Leopold Silver.

He picked up a hand mirror and looked at his face. His nose was covered in heavy sticking plaster. One of his eyes was black and his lips were still swollen. His mother had cried when she saw him. She had come the evening before and brought him a present from his father; a duvet, *the* duvet.

'But I've got a duvet,' Leo had said.

'I know, darling, but he wants you to have this as well.'

'You mean sleep under two duvets? I'd die of heatstroke.'

She surreptitiously touched wood at the mention of death and said, 'A spare.'

'Why didn't he come with you?'

'He won't come to this part of London. He hasn't crossed Oxford Street for two years.'

'Why not?'

'How should I know why (*vy*) not? I'm only married to him.'

He'd given up. He'd keep the duvet for a week or so in case his father wanted it back for some arcane reason, then he'd make a present of it to Oxfam.

Zoe came into the room with coffee. 'It's instant,' she said. 'Sorry about that but we've run out of the real stuff. How're you feeling?'

'I'm OK.'

'Leo, have you thought yet?'

'What about?'

'Are you going to sue?'

'Who?'

'The police, of course.'

'Why? I was on duty. The driver didn't do it on purpose.'

'I know but two road accidents in a week are ridiculous.'

'That's life,' he said, letting the lie mature.

And life was something else too, he thought. It was a stone dropped in a pond that produced a series of remorseless, unstoppable wavelets, each one linked to the next. So if the car crash was the dropped stone then all that had happened since was inevitable.

He reached for his volume of Thurber and searched for several minutes. At last he found what he was looking for and read . . . 'even a well-ordered life cannot lead anybody safely around the inevitable doom that waits in the skies . . . the claw of the sea-puss gets us all in the end.'

He couldn't put it better than that and with any luck Zoe would never know the real circumstances.

She put her head round the door and said, 'I'm going out to get a chicken and I'm going to make you chicken soup.'

'I don't like chicken soup.'

'Yes, you do. Anyway it's good for Jewish invalids.'

'I'm not an invalid.'

'But Jewish. Gotcha!'

He lay back. He was still feeling humiliated and shaken. Guilt was part of it and a whole host of other things some of which had to do with justice and injustice.

The injustice done to Laura had been brutal in the extreme. But did you torture because of it? Kill?

He heard Zoe in the kitchen. His life was going on as it always had. But that didn't stop him feeling depressed.

What he had been involved in was a kind of Macrae scenario.

The one thing he didn't want was to become another Macrae.

And he never wanted to meet another psychotic like Laura.

What really bothered him was that he had always thought such things did not happen to him.

Now he had found they did.

Ai
Ki
Do.
Harmony
Energy
And The Way . . . baby . . . The Way . . .

Alan Scholefield
Dirty Weekend £4.99

'London had always meant Hampstead to her. It was still a village, the last remaining village in the megalopolis . . .'

Maria Dunlap only had her marriage to think about when she joined the families, their children and their dogs taking advantage of the Easter sunshine on the Heath.

But underneath the arches of Hungerford Bridge, Detective Superintendent George Macrae and Detective Sergeant Leopold Silver of London's Cannon Row police station had a brutal murder to investigate.

And from one part of London to another, the sinister trail would reach out to entangle Maria Dunlap . . .

'Portraying relationships as adeptly as Reginald Hill and P. D. James, Scholefield offers an example of crime writing at its best'
PUBLISHERS WEEKLY

'An intricate story, cleverly interwoven, with the strong cast headed by an attractive pair of detectives'
THE MAIL ON SUNDAY

'Promising openers for burly Macrae and sensitive Silver'
THE SUNDAY TIMES

Alan Scholefield
Thief Taker £4.99

London on a sunny day in Spring. Lovers were out, and in the parks you had to step over them. Everyone was out. Even the killers . . .

And that, for Detectives George Macrae and Leo Silver, means another murder.

With a convicted felon terrorising Silver and his girlfriend, and Macrae struggling with the residue of two failed marriages, the last thing they need is the discovery of the corpse of a shipping tycoon in his London apartment.

As the murder investigation progresses, it soon becomes clear that Macrae and Silver are not the only ones whose pasts have come back to haunt them . . .

'A morass of badness and madness . . . Scholefield has his cool, compelling way with forms of deviancy, plus a warm eye to the contrasted lifestyles of his two coppers'
SUNDAY TIMES

'Scholefield writes with an assured wry wit . . . a well-plotted story'
EVENING STANDARD

'So gripping that I was feverishly turning the pages till dawn'
DAILY MAIL

Alan Scholefield
Never Die in January £4.99

' "Never die in January, laddie" Macrae said to Silver. "It's a bloody awful month . . ." '

And never borrow money from criminals, he might have added. Because when you're too broke to pay they're liable to ask for something more permanent than interest . . .

Welching on an underworld loan was the latest in the long line of personal disasters for Detective Superintendent George Macrae of Cannon Row police station. Even his sergeant, Leopold Silver, couldn't afford to turn a blind eye.

But then came the blackmail – and the suicide of a beautiful woman; *And the discovery that it was Macrae who was meant to die . . .*

'Third vigorous manifestation of the Cannon Row partnership . . . an object lesson in what can be packed into fewer than 200 raunchy pages'
JOHN COLEMAN, SUNDAY TIMES

'Anyone wanting to feel the collar of the new-style fictional cop should read Alan Scholefield'
EVENING STANDARD

'Grimly effective . . . Alan Scholefield expertly mingles Macrae's plight with parallel plots involving a vengeful woman and juvenile thuggery'
MIKE SNAITH, SUNDAY EXPRESS

'More twists and turns than a getaway car make this a series to relish'
DAILY POST

Alan Scholefield
Threats & Menaces £4.99

'She was lying on her side, legs drawn up. "Get up," he said. But
she couldn't. When he got like this he was uncontrollable. She
could see it in his eyes now. Vacant. Mad. This time she knew
he was going to kill her . . .'

The discovery of a battered body in a luxury apartment block turns a
routine burglary investigation into a murder inquiry for Detective
Superintendent George Macrae and Detective Sergeant Leopold
Silver.

It's all in a day's work for Macrae . . . until the case attracts the
attention of the top brass at M16. How do you solve a murder in
the spotlight when your only witness is a terrified – and confused –
seven-year-old child?

'Scholefield serves up yet another wicked brew of sin and bitters'

All Pan Books are available at your local bookshop or newsagent, or can be ordered direct from the publisher. Indicate the number of copies required and fill in the form below.

Send to: Macmillan General Books C.S.
               Book Service By Post
               PO Box 29, Douglas I-O-M
               IM99 1BQ

or phone: 01624 675137, quoting title, author and credit card number.

or fax: 01624 670923, quoting title, author, and credit card number.

or Internet: http://www.bookpost.co.uk

Please enclose a remittance* to the value of the cover price plus 75 pence per book for post and packing. Overseas customers please allow £1.00 per copy for post and packing.

*Payment may be made in sterling by UK personal cheque, Eurocheque, postal order, sterling draft or international money order, made payable to Book Service By Post.

Alternatively by Access/Visa/MasterCard

Card No. ⬚⬚⬚⬚⬚⬚⬚⬚⬚⬚⬚⬚⬚⬚⬚⬚⬚⬚⬚

Expiry Date ⬚⬚⬚⬚⬚⬚⬚⬚⬚⬚⬚⬚⬚⬚⬚⬚⬚⬚

Signature _____

Applicable only in the UK and BFPO addresses.

While every effort is made to keep prices low, it is sometimes necessary to increase prices at short notice. Pan Books reserve the right to show on covers and charge new retail prices which may differ from those advertised in the text or elsewhere.

NAME AND ADDRESS IN BLOCK CAPITAL LETTERS PLEASE

Name _____

Address _____

_____

_____

_____

8/95

Please allow 28 days for delivery.
Please tick box if you do not wish to receive any additional information. ☐